MY FAIR SCOT

THE MACKENZIES TAKE LONDON, BOOK 1

SARA BENNETT

ARE YOU SIGNED UP FOR DRAGONBLADE'S BLOG?

You'll get the latest news and information on exclusive giveaways, exclusive excerpts, coming releases, sales, free books, cover reveals and more.

Check out our complete list of authors, too!

No spam, no junk. That's a promise!

Sign Up Here

www.dragonbladepublishing.com

Dearest Reader;

Thank you for your support of a small press. At Dragonblade Publishing, we strive to bring you the highest quality Historical Romance from some of the best authors in the business. Without your support, there is no 'us', so we sincerely hope you adore these stories and find some new favorite authors along the way.

Happy Reading!

CEO, Dragonblade Publishing

Additional Dragonblade Books by Author Sara Bennett

The MacKenzies Take London Series
My Fair Scot (Book 1)

Disgraceful Duchesses Series
Seducing the Duchess (Book 1)
Tempting the Duchess (Book 2)
Dalliance with the Duchess (Book 3)

CHAPTER ONE

1815, Bonnyrigg Castle, Scotland

Callum MacKenzie took one last look about him. Bonnyrigg had been his home for only fifteen years of his twenty-five upon this earth, but he had known about it for much longer. When his grandfather, the Duke of Bonnyrigg, had died at the turn of the century, his parents had returned here, as they had long ago promised. It had been a condition of their marrying that they would take over the estate. His father had become the duke, and his mother the duchess, and as the eldest son, Callum would one day take his father's place.

Callum was aware of the gravity of that position. There had been dukes of Bonnyrigg for centuries, and the old duke had squirreled most of his money away, so there was no shortage of funds. The problem was that the Scottish aristocracy looked down upon the MacKenzie family, sneering at their pretensions. His father, Maxwell, had been a lowly gamekeeper who had dared to marry his mother, Luna, the duke's daughter. Although Maxwell was intelligent and clever, and had been more than capable of assuming his new position, his beginnings had not been forgotten, and besides, the pair of them had led a deeply unconventional life before they moved into the castle.

The unmarried daughters of those who should be their equals turned up their noses at the MacKenzie brothers, and yet Callum's parents wanted him to marry someone who would bring favor as well as fortune to the family. Someone well-bred with important connections, who could lift the MacKenzies from their present obscurity and take their rightful position with the rest of the Scottish nobility. Someone who would bolster their Bonnyrigg inheritance.

So the sad fact was, if Callum wanted to find the sort of wife who could satisfy all of those requirements, then he must travel south over the border. He must also gain some polish and learn to be a duke-in-waiting.

He must go to London.

Maxwell drew him into a hard hug. "Take care, my son," he said, his deep voice husky with emotion. "I have high hopes for you. We will show the doubters that the MacKenzies are not to be underestimated."

Next, his mother, Luna, wrapped her arms about him, looking up at her much taller eldest son. "The ladies of London will flock to you. How could they not?"

She was smiling so he smiled back.

His two brothers watched on, Rory yawning after being out all night, and Donal a little anxiously—he and Donal were close. Cat, their sister, held onto a stripy kitten, tears in her eyes. Callum wanted to assure her he would be back home before she knew it, but he didn't trust his voice.

Behind him, his companion on the journey, Angus Grant, steadied his horse and held the reins of Callum's black stallion. It was time for him to leave, but now the moment had arrived, Callum tarried.

He took a deep breath.

"You won't forget—"

"The one hundred things you listed for me not to forget?" his father said, his brown eyes—so like his eldest son's—gleaming with humor. "Don't worry, Callum. Everything will be fine here at Bonnyrigg while you are in London. Time will fly, you will see. Now off you go, son, and bring us back a wife who will impress our neighbors."

The ache in his heart grew more painful, but there was nothing he could do except hope this journey would be over soon and he would return to the place he loved. Hopefully with the sort of well-connected wife his parents wanted. Callum mounted his black stallion—appropriately called Midnight—and turned to the road south. Angus, his friend and manservant and anything else he was required to be, was at his heels.

After half a mile, Callum turned to Angus. "What do you think London is like?"

"Big and noisy," Angus said cheerfully.

Callum knew that Angus, who must be at least forty years old, had been sent south with him because his father trusted the man to keep a close watch on his son. Did he think Callum was not up to the task assigned him? Or was he worried Callum would make a fool of himself and his family in his attempts to attract a mate? Like some sort of awkward Scottish bird far out of his territory.

He wasn't at all sure he wanted to mingle with the English upper classes. They were known liars and prevaricators, and he would be expected to bow and grovel, and Callum was not one to do either if he did not feel mutual respect. He was known far and wide as a man who said what he thought without fear or favor, so he would have to constantly watch his tongue.

"You will get used to London ways," Angus spoke at his side. "Some delight in the place so much they do not want to leave. Enjoy yourself, Callum! It is but a short time out of your life, and who knows, you might even relish prancing about with the ladies."

"You have me confused with Rory," Callum muttered.

Just as Callum was said to be the serious son, Rory cared only for the pursuit of pleasure and entertainment and was rarely home before dawn.

"Besides," he added, "I doubt my aunt will put up with any of that nonsense."

His parents had arranged for him to stay with his mother's sister, Jennie, who was married to the Earl of Strathmore. They had a town house in London and were far more socially engaged than the MacKenzies. At least Jennie would be a friendly face among the sea of strangers, and English strangers at that. He knew Scotland was supposed to be part of the union with England, but he had never been comfortable with it. If he had been born a hundred years earlier, he would have joined the rebels fighting against the German king who had been set upon the throne instead of the Scottish Stuart.

"As well as finding a wife, your father wants you to gain some polish." Angus was still trying to make his task palatable. "When you're the duke, you will need to rub shoulders with the quality whether you want to or not."

As much as he liked Angus, who was no fool—and it would be good to have someone from home at his side—Callum was tired of his optimism.

"I am not one for crowds," he said.

"Mabbe not, but you will have to learn to pretend you are comfortable in situations where you are far from it."

Callum already knew this; he just didn't want to think about it. He turned and gave Angus a look, and the older man snorted a laugh.

"Aye, you are your mother's son all right," he said. "You have the glare."

"I will obey my parents," Callum said stiffly. "I will go to London and seek a wife. But I won't linger."

"As to that—"

"I will give myself two months, Angus. I will be needed at home then for the harvest, and so I will return to Bonnyrigg, wife or no'."

Angus sighed but was wise enough to keep his opinions to himself.

CHAPTER TWO

Jasmyne Street, London

T HE ROOM WAS elegant, as was the woman seated on the chaise longue. Fair hair coiled neatly upon her head, and a plain and yet tasteful plum-colored gown showed off her bosom, but modestly. Penelope Armstrong was a beauty. She might be two years off thirty, but she had the sort of ageless good looks that would serve her well into old age.

Penelope had once been a courtesan, but those days were—thankfully—over. The gentleman who had paid for her to live in a house in Chelsea and put the clothes upon her back had died three years ago. She could have found another protector, but the thought made her dreadfully unhappy. Not so much because her lover had died—he was old after all—but because the life she was leading was not the one she wanted. It was a life she had been forced into through circumstance.

She had long wanted to step away from that awful title of "courtesan," but the truth was she was not trained for any other occupation. Even in normal circumstances, her birth would have made those choices limited—she could choose to be a governess or a companion—but who would employ her when they learned about her past? Though if she was no longer a courtesan, then the future looked stark. How would she afford to eat? And what of her young brother, Mortimer, who was still dependent upon her?

It was her now deceased protector, Lord Muir, who had given her the idea of how she could attain her freedom. One day he had overheard her explaining in detail to another woman—yes, also a courtesan—how she should behave when in the company of aristocratic gentlemen. What to call each of them depending on their title or standing in society, and which of them should receive the deepest curtsy.

Impressed, Lord Muir had declared her a marvel, and only then did it occur to Penelope that she knew things that others didn't. She had been schooled by a first-rate governess up until she had attended a ladies' finishing college, so she had many useful skills when it came to manners, rules, and etiquette, and she was an excellent teacher. Once Lord Muir was dead, and she was considering her future, Penelope remembered that moment. She thought of all the newly wealthy people who desperately wanted to consort with blue-blooded aristocrats or dreamed of mingling in polite society, only to be mocked and refused entry because they did not know even the bare rudiments of acceptable behavior.

They needed help, and it was the sort of help Penelope was qualified to give.

For a fee.

At first, after setting up her business, she had struggled. She was a "fallen woman" after all, and would-be clients were wary. But as word spread, mostly due to the whispers of those who had succeeded because of her tuition, Penelope found herself with plenty of eager pupils. She was not wealthy by any means, but her new occupation meant that she did not lie awake at night worrying where the next meal might come from.

Or at least she would not worry if Mortimer did not keep asking her for money. He was perpetually broke and Penelope had a sick feeling that was only the tip of the iceberg. Her father had been a gambler who had wasted his inheritance, and when he and her mother died in a coach accident, they had left nothing for their eighteen-year-old daughter and eight-year-old son.

It had been up to Penelope to act as both sister and parent.

She had been embarrassed that she had had to take up the

offer of a friend of her father's, and become his mistress, so that she could put food on the table. She had imagined Mortimer was embarrassed, too, and would be pleased and proud that she had now become respectable. Yet something he had said the other day came to mind.

It was better before.

At the time, she had dismissed his words—he had been cross because she could not loan him the full amount he had asked for—but now she wondered. Did he care so little for her reputation that he would push her back into the scandalous life she had escaped, just so he could have more spending money?

She shifted restlessly upon the chaise longue. No, surely her brother would not do such a thing. And yet . . . she loved him dearly, but she was beginning to think she might have spoiled him by always giving way to his demands. Perhaps it was time she said no.

She looked across the room to Selina, her maid and closest friend, who was arranging some flowers in a vase. "What time was the gentleman's appointment?" she asked, with a glance at the ticking clock on the mantel.

"Now!" Selina said with a frown. "I wonder where he is?" She went to peer out of the window that overlooked the street. "There is no one at the door. Perhaps he has changed his mind."

"Changed his mind?" Penelope scoffed. "After the incident at the Yeos', I think he would know he needs all the help he can get."

Selina smiled broadly, her pretty, mature face creasing into familiar lines. She was no longer the young girl who had dressed Penelope's mother, but she had become a dear friend.

Details of the *incident at the Yeos'* had been spread far and wide, and there had been universal wonder and condemnation that the son of the Duke of Bonnyrigg lacked such basic social skills. "Barbarian" was one of the words affixed to him, as well as "brute". It was not a good start for someone who had only just arrived in London.

"Did he really attack the table decoration?" Selina asked, eyes bright. "I wish I could have seen it."

"One of my old school friends was there—the only one who still speaks to me—and she said he believed the stuffed boar was about to run rampant among the guests." Penelope replied in her usual droll manner, but she was grinning too. "I suppose that his actions could have been considered brave. Boars are dangerous, particularly in Scotland. Ellie said that before it happened, the ladies had all been swooning at the sight of him, but now no one will invite him anywhere."

Selina laughed and then gave an enormous shiver. She looked to the hearth and the half empty basket that sat there. "Is that all the coal we have for the fire? It is freezing in here."

"Put more clothes on," Penelope suggested. "We won't get any more coal until next week, and even then I have ordered a lesser quantity. You know how stretched we are at the moment, Selina. I had to loan Mortimer some more money."

The word "loan" hung uncomfortably in the air, and Selina looked as if she would have liked to comment on it. But she knew better than to come between sister and brother, so she remained silent. She was surprised when Penelope, instead of ignoring the subject as she usually did, addressed it.

"I *will* speak to him," Penelope spoke firmly. "I cannot continue to fund his wild habits. As for Uncle Bertie . . . I wish I had never allowed Mortimer to stay with him. Instead of being a sobering influence, he is making matters worse."

Bertie was her mother's brother and called himself an inventor. But his inventions never succeeded and never made any money, and now Mortimer was caught up in Bertie's madcap schemes.

"I think that is for the best," Selina replied cautiously.

She had been Penelope's maid and companion for ten years and understood her better than anyone. When Penelope's mother had died, Selina had agreed to come to live with Penelope in the house in Chelsea, where she resided as Lord Muir's mistress.

Selina had seen for herself the struggles of her young mistress and was glad when she left that life behind. It was just a pity Mortimer had battened himself on his sister. Selina knew Penelope still thought of him as the little boy she had comforted all those years ago, when he had wept for their lost parents, but he had grown into a most unpleasant young man.

"We have had a lucrative year so far," Penelope was saying. "There were the two Hanbury sisters who could barely manage a curtsy."

"Mill owner's daughters," Selina said disparagingly. "You whipped them into shape in no time."

Penelope smiled with satisfaction and tapped a fingertip on *The Times* which lay on the table in front of her. "I was just reading that one of them is now engaged to a titled gentleman."

"Let's hope she does not keep you a secret."

"And then there was the Fotheringham boy. Remember how he blushed every time he saw a girl and stammered when he asked one to dance? His mother sent me a very nice note when he excelled at Almack's."

"You worked miracles," Selina agreed proudly. "You always do."

Penelope looked pleased with herself, the worry line between her brows vanishing now they had moved away from talk of her wretched brother. "I do, don't I, Selina?"

"This new client we are waiting on is a duke's son, is that right? Does he have a title?"

"Indeed he does. He is the Marquess of Morven. Although no title will help him if he keeps attacking table decorations." She drew her shawl closer about her and gave the hearth a longing look. The fire had dwindled to a mere flicker.

Selina took her cue and went to the basket and began to add more coal. Immediately, the fire began to smoke badly, the room filling with the putrid clouds. She tried to remove the coal she had just added, to remedy the problem, but it was the chimney that was at fault. Selina was coughing now, and so was Penelope, holding her shawl to her mouth.

"Why didn't I have the chimney cleaned last week when I had the chance?" she cried. The sweep had come to the door, but she had been economizing and sent him away again.

"Because Mortimer needed some money to buy a part for the latest invention," Selina muttered under her breath, and then coughed violently as she breathed in more smoke.

Just then, the door knocker banged loudly from the street below.

Selina wailed. "Is that him? Whatever shall we do?"

Penelope wafted a hand in front of her face. "Let him in, of course! Hurry, Selina, before he goes away."

Selina set off at a quick trot, and a moment later Penelope heard voices, one of them deep and Scottish. It was him. She tried to wave some of the smoke away with her copy of *The Times*, but it did little to clear the air.

Heavy footsteps on the stairs and then there he was. The Marquess of Morven. Tall and broad shouldered with wild dark hair. And handsome, good God, so very handsome. Her eyes widened, watery though they were, and she gave another little cough.

After one swift glance around the room, the marquess strode to the window and thrust it open. Then he went to the fireplace and proceeded to rectify the smoking fire by putting it out completely. As he knelt on the hearth, Penelope had the chance to take a good look at him. He was tall, yes, and broad across the shoulders, but his jacket did not fit him at all well, and the pantaloons he was wearing bagged about the knees. He would have looked much smarter if he were dressed by a reputable tailor. His boots were shiny, there was that, but as he rose to his feet and turned, wiping his sooty hands on his thighs, she could see his necktie was badly arranged, despite the rather nice sapphire pin securing it.

His eyes were brown, the light tea shade of brown she had always admired, and his dark hair was too long and too untidy.

He looked as if when he got up this morning, his valet—if he had one—had not bothered to even attempt to make him look presentable.

"You need your chimney cleaned, mistress," he announced, his voice deep.

"I know."

He cocked a dark brow at her.

"Never mind that," she said briskly. She was standing, but she had to look up at him, because he was at least a foot taller than her. "You are the Marquess of Morven, I presume?"

"I am," he said.

She waited for him to bow or take her hand, but he stood and stared down at her like he had all the time in the world. Hmm, there was work to be done here, and work meant she would be paid. Again, she admitted to herself how desperately she needed the money.

Penelope glanced over at the door and saw Selina lingering. Her maid's eyes were wide with a mixture of anxiety and glee.

"Fetch tea, Selina," Penelope said in her well-modulated voice. "I believe the marquess will be staying."

CHAPTER THREE

SHE WAS THE most beautiful woman he had ever seen. Her hair was as fair as the moon, and her eyes were the sort of silvery grey he had only heard of in folktales where fairies danced around toadstools and put spells on unwary travelers. Now the fire had stopped smoking, Callum had nothing to occupy him to help recover his wits—the sight of her had scattered them to the four winds—so he was glad when she had ordered her servant to bring tea.

"My name is Penelope Armstrong," she said, holding out a delicate hand.

Callum took it and gave it a squeeze. She winced so he let it go.

"Please be seated," she said, gesturing at a chair, and sat herself down on the delicate looking settee.

He did as he was told, a little too enthusiastically, and the chair groaned under his weight. She was watching him but he wasn't sure what she wanted, so he waited. People usually told him what they wanted eventually, and it saved him guessing or filling the silence with unnecessary chatter.

"Perhaps you should tell me why you are here, my lord?" she said at last.

Callum thought it was obvious but told her anyway. "My aunt suggested I come to you. She gave me the time and the place and here I am."

Miss Armstrong nodded and waited, and then said, "And the

reason you are here, my lord?"

Memories of that fateful evening at the Yeos' made him want to kick something, but instead, he glared. "Evidently I am not fit for polite society, or that is what I have been told. The invitations have dried up. I am supposed to be in London to . . ." He stopped. Was it polite to mention wanting a noble wife? Callum liked to say what he thought, and second guessing himself was proving difficult.

His aunt had sighed and cast her eyes up when he told her what happened with the boar. But she didn't agree that he should return home to Bonnyrigg immediately, as Callum had hopefully suggested. She seemed to think that lessons were in order. Callum resisted. He wasn't about to turn himself into a dandy. If he found a wife, then she would have to take him as he was. Aunt Jennie had retorted that she would write to his parents and tell them he was being ungrateful and stubborn, and only then did he agree to the appointment with Penelope Armstrong.

Miss Armstrong was watching him curiously. "Tell me, my lord, why do you want invitations? What has brought you to London during the Season?"

Frustrated, he ran his hands through his hair and straightened in his chair. "I need a wife. A wife who can impress our noble neighbors. I've come south to find one."

She blinked those remarkable eyes at him. "I see. If you want to attract such a wife, then you will need to court her. Woo her. You have arrived in the capital just as the Season is getting into full swing, and there are a great many young women making their coming-outs. They will want a man who is polite and courteous, who will make them feel special. I am not sure you are that man."

Was that an insult? "I can be polite and courteous," he argued.

"You are intimidating," she said firmly. Before he could argue further, she added, "Let me be frank, my lord. I think you are a man who prefers plain speaking, as I do. I find it saves time."

Relieved, he agreed. "Honesty is important to me."

"Very well then. The young women making their debuts are innocent virgins, and even if they are not, they will be playing that role. It is likely that when they meet you, they will be overwhelmed by your . . . manliness."

His *manliness*? He raised his eyebrows, surprised and not displeased. "What is wrong with that? Is my 'manliness' a problem?"

"Not for some ladies. A widow, for instance, might welcome a gentleman who exudes masculinity. There are many widows of noble gentlemen, and having been wed once already, they may not be as particular when it comes to your lack of social skills. Although some widows are *very* particular."

He thought a moment. "Can *I* be frank now, Miss Armstrong? It doesn't matter to me who I marry. I have no preference as long as she is happy to come and live at Bonnyrigg with me."

She looked doubtful. "Well, we'll get to that. For now, you need to receive invitations, otherwise how will you enter polite society and find your wife?"

"That is why I am here," he said a trifle impatiently.

"Yes, you need my help, my lord."

"Enough with the 'my lords'," he burst out, raising his voice. "I am Callum MacKenzie, and that was my name until I turned 14, so you can call me Callum or MacKenzie, either will do."

She gave him one of her inscrutable looks. "I see. Your aunt said you are in line for a dukedom."

"Did she? Well, my father is hale and hearty, so I won't be a duke for a good while yet. Is that a problem?"

She shook her head. "No, of course not."

"So my title is not a problem?"

"It is an advantage. The problem is you do not know how to behave in society, and although the society hostesses will turn a blind eye to many things in order to get a marquess through their doors, they will not put up with bad manners."

Callum was beginning to wish Penelope Armstrong were not

quite so frank. But she was not yet finished.

"And there is more to it than your lack of manners, I'm afraid. Your appearance needs work too, my . . . MacKenzie. How long will you be staying in London before you must return to Bonnyrigg?"

"I prefer not to stay too long," he said. "I find it . . ."

At that moment the maid arrived with the tea tray. She was older than her mistress, rather tall and thin, with hair the color of a hay bale. She gave him a wicked little smile that made Callum wonder if she had been eavesdropping at the door just before she entered.

"Thank you, Selina," Miss Armstrong said calmly. "Leave us now, if you please."

Obediently, the maid bobbed a curtsy and left. Penelope began to pour tea, asking how he preferred it, and setting his cup and saucer down closer to his chair. There was cake, too, but Callum thought it looked like some strange English concoction and refused her offer of a piece.

"The first thing you must learn is that people don't really care what you think. You may be desperate to return to Scotland, but if you tell people that, they will find you boorish." She stopped, realizing her misstep in referencing a certain boar, and changed the word to, "*Ill-mannered.* When they ask you how you are enjoying London, tell them you are enjoying it very much. Wax lyrically about the sights and how much you prefer it to where you came from."

"So if I am not to appear *boorish* or ill-mannered, I should lie," Callum said sarcastically.

"Yes, if you want to put it like that. *Lying* will make you more friends and get you more invitations."

"My aunt is holding a ball in three weeks," he said, aware he sounded as if that was the worst thing he could imagine.

"Three weeks!" Her voice was a little shrill. She took a breath and relaxed the hands clutched in her lap. "Well, I suppose if you work hard . . ." Her eyes narrowed as they ran over him, and suddenly Callum felt very self-conscious. Angus had tried to tell him he looked like a rag bag, but he had ignored him. As long as he was comfortable in his attire, what did it matter what anyone else thought? But he realized now that it *did* matter. To Penelope Armstrong, it mattered very much.

He picked up the delicate cup in his fist and took a gulp of his tea, trying not to notice her eyes watching his every move. Dear God, was this what it was going to be like for the next three weeks? Was his every word and move going to be judged and found wanting? He longed to go home, to stand in the forests around Bonnyrigg, and breathe in the clean air and listen to the sounds of birds and animals, while the wind stirred through the branches.

But he had been sent south on a mission, and he must try his very best to succeed.

"Three weeks will be long enough," he assured her. "I am a fast learner."

She took a sip of her tea and let his words pass without comment. "We should fix on a fee," she said, and set down her cup with a gentle clink before she named a price that made his eyes water. But he held his nerve. His Aunt Jennie had said she had heard from several of her friends who were acquainted with people who had used such services, and that Penelope Armstrong was the best, and to get the best one must pay. It would be worth it if in two months he was heading home with a wife.

"Are we agreed?" She was watching him again, those pixie eyes seeming to see right through him. Disconcerting, but also mesmerizing.

Callum smiled. He had been told he had a very nice smile.

She blinked.

"We are agreed," he said and rose and held out his hand.

She rose, too, and her hand vanished within his much larger grip. This time he did not squeeze. "I will see you tomorrow morning at ten," she said, in a no-nonsense voice that made him feel strangely squirmy inside. "Be prepared to stay for the entire day."

"Do you think a day will be enough then?"

She laughed. "I do not. Goodbye, my . . . MacKenzie."

He bowed and left the room. Outside, the maid showed him to the door, her gaze sliding over him in a curious manner. She leaned in just as he turned to leave.

"Don't you worry," she said, "Miss Armstrong will have you pulled into line in no time at all. And people have short memories. There will be another scandal to take the place of yours." She stopped, aware that she might have overstepped the mark.

"Thank you," Callum said with amusement. Then, curiously, "Is Miss Armstrong married?"

Selina's eyes widened. "I think you will find the answer to that is in her title. *Miss*."

"Is she engaged then?"

"No, she is not. She is single and has no plans to change her state."

"Hmm." He nodded, deep in thought, and as he stepped outside, he heard the door close behind him. The beautiful Penelope Armstrong was not married nor about to be, and he wondered why not. She should have suitors lining up for miles. If he could find a wife like her, he would consider himself a very lucky man.

But then he remembered her watchful gaze, as if she had found him wanting. Could he gain her approval? Could he change the way those remarkable eyes lingered on him? For some reason, Miss Armstrong's good opinion now seemed far more important to him than that of the English lords and ladies he had come to impress.

Deep in thought, Callum set off back to his aunt's house in Mayfair.

CHAPTER FOUR

"HE AGREED TO pay how much?" Selina exclaimed breathlessly, eyes shining as they met her mistress's. "I can't believe he didn't quibble!"

"Nor can I. I was certain he would. Now we can order more coal." Penelope was so relieved. "But for goodness sake, don't say anything to my brother," she added and then felt guilty. But it was true, if Mortimer heard of her good fortune with her new client, he would tell Uncle Bertie, and then they would be around in a flash begging for more funds. She was aware that the time had come to refuse him, but not today. She did not want to spoil her good mood.

"How long do you have to turn MacKenzie into a gentleman?" Selina asked with a doubtful look.

Penelope grimaced. "His aunt is holding a ball in his honor in three weeks. I don't think I can do it. And yet I must!"

"Yes, you must," Selina gave her a long look. "He's very handsome. Pity you're not in the market for a husband. Training him to be a gentleman could take a lifetime."

Penelope pulled a face. "I am afraid I am not respectable enough for him."

Just for a moment she allowed herself to think of it—MacKenzie as part of her life. He was the sort of man who appealed to her, in particular his "manliness". When he had smiled at her just now! She didn't want to admit it even to herself, but she missed the intimacy of her relationship with Lord Muir.

He had been older and it hadn't been often that he took her to bed, but when he had, she'd found such pleasure in the joining of their flesh. The three years since he had died had meant three years alone.

There had been no one else. She had considered it, but it seemed chancy to take a lover and risk her growing popularity among the people she was trying to persuade to hire her as a society tutor. They might forgive a fallen woman, but only if that woman sought redemption by turning her back on her past.

Now the thought of MacKenzie was stirring up all the wicked feelings she had been trying to suppress.

Aware of Selina watching her with knowing eyes, she searched for something else to say to distract her clever friend.

"I have three weeks to get MacKenzie ready for his aunt's ball, and if that is successful, perhaps I can offer to help him find a suitable wife. That would mean more fees and fill up the coffers even more."

"Why do you think he chose us?"

"His aunt is the Countess of Strathmore. She arranged the appointment for her nephew. She had heard that my success in bringing my clients up to scratch was unparalleled."

Selina looked like she was going to wonder aloud whether this might turn out to be her first failure but obviously thought better of it.

Penelope knew she could not afford to fail.

When her parents had been killed, Penelope had learned that what she had always thought of as her settled and comfortable life was an illusion. She was just eighteen and due to make her come-out, but it had been delayed. Her father had made plenty of excuses and she had accepted them, but once he was gone she had found out the truth. The family were in serious debt. They were about to lose everything.

How would she look after Mortimer, her young brother? How would she look after herself?

Her only living relative—her grandparents were dead—was

her Uncle Bertie, her mother's brother, but he was a scatter-brained fellow more interested in his inventions than his niece and nephew. There was only one other person interested in helping. Lord Muir. He was an old friend of the family, or so she had always believed. He had called upon her to offer, so she thought, his condolences, but that meeting had not gone as expected.

He said he would help her financially if she became his mistress.

Once the shock had worn off, practical Penelope did not see that she had any choice. She could not take a position as a governess or companion, not when she had her eight-year-old brother to care for, and placing him in an orphanage was not something she could contemplate. And actually, Lord Muir was quite handsome in a mature sort of way, with his greying hair and the lines around his eyes from smiling. She knew him, and she trusted him.

She had said yes to his proposal.

Penelope understood now how naïve she had been, how unworldly. Lord Muir had been kind to her, generous even, but their relationship had not been one of love. It had been convenient. She needed his help, and he needed someone he could pay intimate visits to. He had never had any intention of marrying her. He was a widower, and his marriage had been unhappy and not something he wanted to repeat. Penelope had done what was asked of her, ignoring the disapproval of her old friends and the avoidance of her peers. Tucked away in the house in Chelsea, her days had dragged. At times she had been intolerably lonely. Soon her longing to escape her claustrophobic life had grown almost unbearable.

And now that she had escaped, she would not be going back.

She shook her head. Today, she would not think of the past. Today, her future was looking bright. MacKenzie—or, more formally, the Marquess of Morven—was the highest ranked gentleman she had ever been asked to help enter polite society.

Yes, she was a little nervous about the three-week deadline, but she could do it. She *must* do it, if she wanted to be paid.

Selina was seated on a chair, watching her with interest and waiting for her instructions. Whenever there was a new client, Penelope liked to plan her training schedule, and Selina had been a wonderful support since Penelope had thrown herself into this new venture. If, sometimes, she bemoaned the fact that Penelope was still single then it was best to ignore her. Some people were not designed for marriage and a happy ever after, and Penelope concluded she was one of them.

She picked at a slice of cake as she considered her next step. "I think we should start tomorrow with the formalities around the serving and the eating of a meal. What do you think?"

Selina laughed. "Should I serve boar?"

Penelope considered the question seriously. "No. He might believe we are sniggering at his misfortune. Besides, I am quite sure he knows how he went wrong and is not likely to repeat it."

"Soup, then? That can be problematic for someone not used to formal dining. Surely he will not expect a four course meal?"

"No. Just soup and dessert will do. We can always expand the menu if necessary."

"Syllabub?" Selina asked with a wicked smile. "That's always tricky."

"Exactly. Raspberry syllabub, I think. That should do it. We will eat, and afterward I will tell him where he went wrong, and what he needs to practice. Then I suppose we should move on to appearance. His hair was rather long."

"But very nice all the same," Selina said a little dreamily.

Penelope ignored her. "And did you see his neckcloth? Not to mention his jacket and pantaloons. He looked like he was off to fight ten rounds in a pugilism contest . . ." She stopped because the image of MacKenzie shaping up for a fight, all focus and muscle, had distracted her.

"Or like he had just rolled out of bed," Selina added.

That thought was even more distracting. Penelope went on

smoothly, as though she were not plagued by visions of a naked MacKenzie. "Does he have a valet? I doubt it."

"It certainly looked as if he didn't care what you thought of him."

"He'll care after tomorrow."

Selina smiled a secretive smile. "Yes, I think he will be looking for your approval."

Penelope wasn't so sure. There was something about Callum MacKenzie that made her think he would not be an easy man to master. She had caught a glint of stubborn resistance in his brown eyes. He might claim he wanted to succeed, but it was not always easy to turn yourself into someone else. She knew that only too well.

"If MacKenzie wants to find himself a well-bred wife then he will have to do as I say."

"I have a feeling he will be eager to please," Selina said.

There was something sly about her expression that Penelope wasn't sure she liked. Did her maid have a secret she wasn't sharing? Sometimes, with Selina, it was better not to know.

CALLUM REACHED HIS aunt's home and gave the knocker a forceful rattle. Hocking, the butler, a sour-faced fellow, barely acknowledged him as he opened the door, but Callum was used to it. He was a barbarian, a Scot, and there were plenty of Englishmen like Hocking who neither trusted him nor wanted to know him better.

That would change, he hoped, once Penelope Armstrong taught him the rudimentary skills he needed to enter polite society. It wasn't necessary for him to be the perfect picture of a gentleman—indeed, as a rough and ready Highlander, he was very sure he would never attain that standard. He just needed to become a reasonable prospect for the wife of his choosing.

But that was the trouble, because as soon as he had laid eyes on Miss Armstrong, he had wanted *her*, and Callum could be stubborn and determined when it came to something he wanted. Why was she teaching etiquette and manners when she could be putting them into practice in drawing rooms all over London? Was there a reason she was not already married? He needed to discover more about her, and he thought his Aunt Jennie might be able to help with that.

He expected to find Jennie in the parlor, busy at her desk. She liked to deal with her correspondence in the mornings, before callers began knocking on her door or she went to make calls of her own. After spending her early married life in Edinburgh, she had taken to London society like a duck to water, and seemed completely at home.

Luna, Jennie's sister, was very different. She and Callum's father Maxwell had preferred a free and unfettered existence. Maxwell might have been a gamekeeper, but he could turn his hand to many other trades, and so he had in the years the family had traveled about Scotland. Callum had learned to love nature and to feel at one with it. Returning to Bonnyrigg and living such a different life had been hard for them all, but it was the promise they had made to Callum's grandfather, and so they had kept their word.

Bonnyrigg might have been a far different life from roaming the countryside, but Callum still had his freedom. He could get up in the morning and set off to wander about all day, not returning until nightfall. He had always thought of his growing up years as perfect, and it was only now that he realized how woefully unprepared he was for the position he would one day inherit. How could he ever feel comfortable in the drawing rooms of aristocrats? Now, Penelope Armstrong was a different matter. He could imagine her at Bonnyrigg, charming the crusty old nobles who had been friends with his grandfather but looked down upon Maxwell and Luna and their children. He could see her hosting dinner parties in the great hall where even the King wouldn't feel out of place.

But he was getting ahead of himself.

He peeped around the door and found Jennie at her desk.

"Callum!" She smiled as she rose and stretched up to kiss his cheek. She was not like Luna, having fair hair instead of red, and grey eyes instead of blue. Not the silvery grey of Penelope Armstrong, however—again, her image popped into his head and he spent a moment admiring it.

"Do tell me how it all went," Jennie said. "Was Miss Armstrong as clever as everyone says? I wasn't sure at first, with her reputation, but my friends all thought she was the best option for you. She turned Mr. Hanbury's daughters into ladies in the blink of an eye."

Callum didn't know who Mr. Hanbury's daughters were, but he suspected they shared the same ambitions as himself, and were eager to enter society while being completely unsuited to do so. Just how many misfits had Penelope turned into successes?

"Miss Armstrong has agreed to take me on as her client. I start tomorrow at ten o'clock in the morning."

Jennie clasped her hands. "Oh, that is good news!"

Callum gave her a curious look. "What do you mean *with her reputation*, Aunt Jennie?"

His aunt looked surprised. "I thought you knew, but of course, how could you?" She laughed a little nervously. "Penelope Armstrong was the mistress of Lord Muir, until he died three years ago. She was never vulgar, you must not think that. She was brought up as a lady. I'm not sure why she decided to accept his lordship's indecent proposal, but she did. After he died, I believe she had plenty of similar offers, but instead of accepting any of them, she decided to become a teacher of manners and etiquette."

A wrinkle appeared between her brows. "People were a little dubious about her at first, and naturally there was some resistance amongst the more upright members of society, but she seems to have won over all but the most moral of them.

Although socially, she is not invited to go amongst any but the Bohemian set; she would not be welcome."

He was surprised by the news, and yet it explained why she was teaching rather than mingling. Callum tried to picture Penelope Armstrong as some gentleman's mistress and found it made him twitchy. He reminded himself that he had wanted to know about her past, to understand her, but now he asked himself what had led such a beautiful and sophisticated woman to agree to be some man's mistress. And then to reject all the offers that came after he died. Did that mean he had been the love of her life?

Callum's spirits sank.

"But you do like her?" Jennie was eyeing him consideringly.

"She is very . . ." He changed his mind about waxing lyrical about her and stuck with a plain, "Yes, Aunt Jennie, I like her."

But Jennie must have heard something in his voice because her eyes narrowed and she asked, "What *is* her appearance? I have never met her, and I am curious."

Callum chose his words carefully. "She is about my age, I would guess, although she has the manner of someone older. Her hair is fair, very pale, and her eyes are almost silver. She reminds me of the fairytales my father sometimes tells." He smiled. "The sort of tales where the otherworldly creature puts a spell on the mortal, and he pines away with love for her."

He must have gone too far because Jennie looked alarmed. "Well, that sounds a little concerning. Be careful she does not put a spell on you, Callum. Your mother would never forgive me."

Callum laughed. "Don't worry. I am too canny for that."

Jennie didn't look entirely convinced, but she moved the subject on. "I have heard her fees are quite steep. What is she asking?"

Callum had thought that most London ladies thought it vulgar to discuss anything to do with money, but his aunt was a shrewd Scotswoman. When he told her, she seemed taken aback for a moment and then she took a breath and said, "Well, I suppose she can charge whatever she likes after the Hanbury sisters. The change in them was remarkable."

Callum suddenly felt guilty. His aunt had offered to pay the fee as it was she who made the appointment. "Are you sure you can afford such a sum, Aunt Jennie? I can write to Father and ask him—"

"No, don't do that. I can afford it. Strathmore's shipping business has been very lucrative of late. And with no children of my own, I am more than happy to spend my money on my sister's brood."

Jennie had always been kind and generous, and they all loved her. Callum smiled warmly back. "Then thank you. I promise you it will be money well spent. In three weeks, when you hold the ball, you will not know me."

"I hope it is not as drastic as that," she said. "Remember, I love you as you are, nephew. But with just a wee bit of polish, you will be irresistible to all the ladies."

Would he? Callum found himself hoping he would be irresistible to Penelope Armstrong. He sensed that beneath that cool, well-mannered exterior was a woman with hidden depths, and he was eager to plumb them.

CHAPTER FIVE

I T WAS THE following day, and Selina had served the meal. Although Callum had partaken of his usual hearty breakfast only three hours ago, he had no trouble sitting down and eating again. Penelope was seated opposite him, watching closely as her maid delivered and removed plates when necessary.

"You might consider a smaller serving, MacKenzie," Penelope said, her silver eyes narrowed as he ladled more soup into his dish.

"What if I am hungry?"

"Then eat something before you leave your house. You don't want to be thought greedy."

"A greedy Highland barbarian," Callum muttered. "How is this helping me find a well-bred wife?"

"You might find a wife whatever your manners, but if you want one with intelligence and breeding, who is good company and will do you proud as your future duchess, then you need to listen and learn."

There was nothing he could say to that.

"Selina, bring the raspberry syllabub."

A delicate dish was set before him, with the addition of a tiny dessert spoon. Callum picked up the spoon. It was lost in his great paw and he fumbled a moment, finding it necessary to hold it with the tips of his fingers and then take a heaped spoonful of the syllabub and bring it to his lips. It fell off, sliding down his clean shirt in a splodge of raspberry red. He jumped up with a curse and tried to wipe it off with his napkin, only to make the mess on the white linen worse.

Behind him, Selina made a sound that could have been a laugh, but when he turned to glare at her, her face was expressionless.

Penelope was also on her feet. "I think we will forego the syllabub," she said drolly. "It is clearly not what you are used to."

"I prefer my puddings large and solid," he retorted. "And my spoons man-sized."

They looked at each other a moment in silence and then Penelope's lips trembled into a smile, which made him burst into laughter. When he had recovered, he said, "For God's sake, woman, no more syllabub! In fact, no more food. I promise you I willna attack table decorations. I have learned my lesson."

Penelope had been watching him as if she wasn't quite sure what to make of him, but now she said in a firm voice, "I am very glad to hear it. I have a reputation to maintain."

She gave Selina a nod and the woman made haste to clear the table.

"Let us move on to the more general subject of manners. You should not call me "woman". You should address me as Miss Armstrong."

He sighed. He knew this, he wasn't a fool, but all he replied was, "Yes, Miss Armstrong."

"And I should address you as my lord, or my lord Marquess."

"What if I want you to call me MacKenzie? Surely it is up to me what you call me."

"In private perhaps, but in company we should stick to the formalities. People might think it odd if I call you MacKenzie and you call me woman. Let us not confuse everyone."

He nodded. He understood, but the sooner he was done with this, done with London, and on his way home to Bonnyrigg, the better.

Callum looked down at his shirt. The syllabub had soaked through and was sticking to him, and he eased it away from his skin with a grimace. "I need to change. Are we finished, or is there more?"

Penelope wrinkled her brow. "There is more, but I don't suppose you are comfortable like that." She hesitated before she said, "Remove your shirt and Selina will sponge it clean."

Callum looked from one woman to the other and then shrugged. He was used to being shirtless at home, when the weather was warm enough, or when he had built up a sweat, so it did not matter to him one way or the other. But he had never been shirtless in front of two ladies before. It occurred to him that it might be fun to ruffle Penelope's composure. So far he had seen very little of what went on beneath her serene exterior, apart from that one smile that showed him she actually had a sense of humor. He wanted to know more.

With a few tugs, he removed his neckcloth and tossed it aside, and then shrugged off his jacket and set that aside, too. He pulled his soiled shirt over his head and held it out to Selina. She took it, but her gaze was fastened on his bare chest like she had never seen one before. Perhaps she hadn't.

"Ah, thank you, Mr. . . . my . . . MacKenzie."

She whipped around and was out of the door before he could respond. He turned back to Penelope, who quickly lifted her gaze up to his. There was color in her cheeks that hadn't been there before.

"Should we continue?" Callum asked sweetly, with an arch of his dark brow. "We only have three weeks until the ball."

She looked away then back again, being careful to keep her gaze above his neck. "Hmm, very true. Let us pretend you are calling upon a respectable lady and have just been shown into her drawing room."

Penelope seemed even more composed now he was half naked, but he suspected she was not. His bare chest had shaken her somehow, which seemed strange when she must have seen Lord Muir's chest many times. Callum decided to play along and pretend not to notice. He strode to the door and then turned and held out his hand. "How do you do, Respectable Lady. Are you well? What a marvelous day we are having."

Penelope blinked as she stepped forward to take his hand. "You overwhelm me, MacKenzie. I am well, and it is indeed a marvelous day, although I believe it may rain before luncheon. How are you enjoying London?"

Callum was still holding her hand, and strangely he didn't want to let it go. She gave a little tug to remind him to release her. "London is not Bonnyrigg," he said gloomily, and then remembering himself, added, "but I am enjoying it. Aye, it is bonny."

Penelope sat down and gestured for him to do the same. Callum lowered himself to the chair and crossed one booted leg over the other.

There was a pause. She was fiddling with one of the cushions at her side, and he could see she had made a hole in the fabric. Was he making her nervous? He had not thought her the anxious type, but maybe he had been mistaken. Or was it his chest she was nervous about?

He looked down and saw that there was a raspberry streak across his stomach. He ran his finger over it, sucking the dessert into his mouth.

When he looked up, Penelope was watching him with wide eyes, her mouth slightly ajar. So he did it again, taking his time. She gave a little gasp and suddenly jumped up and moved to the window. Surprised, Callum observed her straight back and the way her shoulders stiffened. Against the light from the window, her fashionable dress was opaque and he found himself wishing it was one of those almost transparent ones that Rory had told him the more Bohemian ladies were wearing. Then he would have been able to see right through it.

Ungentlemanly of him, he knew, but lust was rearing its head and he was forgetting to be cautious. Could he touch her? There must be some legitimate way in which he could do that, because suddenly he wanted to feel the texture and warmth of her skin against his fingers. He wanted to feel her soft body pressed to his.

His voice when he spoke was a little sly. "My aunt wants me to be able to dance or at least manage a few turns around the room. Can we do that now?"

"We will get to that," she said, still with her back to him.

"Why don't we start now?" he asked. "While Selina is cleaning my shirt?"

Penelope looked at him over her shoulder and her face wore a suspicious look. Did she suspect him of teasing her? Did she know how much he wanted to take her into his arms? Callum smiled.

Instinctively, she smiled back and then just as quickly wiped it from her face. "You think yourself very clever, do you not, MacKenzie?"

"Aye, I do."

She took a breath. "I have met men like you before," she said evenly. "There is nothing you can say that will surprise me."

"You havena met any men like me," he assured her, and his voice was as smooth as hers. "And I am sure I can surprise you, if you let me."

There was a silence and he wondered if he had gone too far. Would she reprimand him? He rather looked forward to that— her stern voice was very attractive. But he had underestimated her ability to put him in his place.

Penelope gave him a cool, polite smile, and said, as if their previous conversation had never happened, "Tell me a little about your home, MacKenzie. Have you any brothers or sisters?"

"I have two brothers and one sister," he said, happy to follow her lead.

She murmured something he didn't catch, but which sounded like "There are more of them", just as Selina returned with his shirt. It was still a little damp but clean at least. Callum thanked her and pulled it on, leaving the neck open as he shrugged into his jacket.

Penelope breathed what sounded like a sigh of relief, which

nearly made him take it off again, but he resisted.

"Let us practice dancing now," she said. "Selina, the piano if you please!"

CHAPTER SIX

P ENELOPE WAS ANNOYED with herself. What on earth was the
matter with her? She was shaken to the core in a way she
had not been since she was seventeen and introduced to the new
curate at her local parish church. He had been a little older than
her and fair of hair and face, and she had thought she was in love.
Well, in something. Looking back on the experience with
hindsight, she suspected she might have been in lust.

Was that what was happening now? Was she in lust with
MacKenzie? Yes, he was handsome—he was possibly the most
handsome man she had ever encountered, barring the angelic
curate, although in a far more down to earth way—but he was a
client. She never allowed clients to fluster her, and she did not
engage with them in any way but a professional one. She
certainly had never allowed them to disconcert her to the point
where she had to run across the room just to get some breathing
space.

She suspected he knew exactly what he was doing. That
innocent look did not fool her. Was he attracted to her? She had
had that happen before, too, men flirting with her when she was
supposed to be teaching them etiquette. She always put a stop to
it quickly but politely, and if they persisted, then she would
terminate their agreement. It had not happened often, but it had
happened.

Just because she had been Lord Muir's mistress, they seemed
to believe she would agree to anything they suggested. As if she

were vulnerable to every male looking for a brief affair. It made her feel hurt and angry, but she refused to let it show. She did not give them the satisfaction.

If this current situation persisted then she should tell Callum MacKenzie to leave or else she could give him a warning—she suspected a warning would do the trick. Despite his rough and ready ways, he had been cooperative. Why then did she hesitate to do that? And why, when he had smiled at her, did something in her chest turn over giddily? She was twenty-eight, for goodness' sake! She knew better than to fall in lust with a handsome man, especially when she was relying upon his money to pay her bills.

Selina had begun to play the piano softly, clearly not wanting to interrupt Penelope's musings. Selina seemed taken with MacKenzie too, which made sense. Despite his faults, he was rather charming and certainly charismatic, and she did not think it was going to be difficult for him to find a wife. But was that any reason for Penelope to feel as if the ground was shifting beneath her feet in such a ridiculous manner? When he had stripped off his shirt so casually and bared his chest . . . Penelope had felt an almost unstoppable urge to reach out and run her hands over the delicious curves and hollows of his torso. She had wanted to lean in and take his rosy nipples into her mouth and drag her fingers through the dark hair that swept down in a line to his stomach and vanished beneath his pantaloons.

Thank goodness she had more self-control than to give in to her urges!

She guessed it was her longing for intimate contact that had caused her common sense to waver. Her heart was pounding, and her blood was pumping, and her body felt overheated. There was also an embarrassing moistness between her thighs that made her want to squirm in her seat.

Selina kept shooting little glances at her and biting her lip, wanting to smile but knowing she should not. Penelope's situation might be amusing to her friend, but Selina's smiles would soon evaporate if they lost their lucrative client.

Despite her scattered thoughts, Callum MacKenzie was still talking, and she remembered she had asked him to tell her about himself. After his first few words, she had barely heard him, and yet somehow she was managing to carry on a sensible conversation while simultaneously imagining herself unbuttoning his pantaloons and lifting up her skirts, and sitting astride him. Sinking down, down, onto his shaft until it filled her completely.

Penelope gave an audible swallow.

"My brother Rory thinks himself a sophisticated man about town." Callum grimaced. "*I* think he is a conceited show off. My youngest brother Donal is more like me. There's a girl at home he's loved for years, but he's too blate to tell her."

"Too 'blate'?" she repeated, managing to regain her wits.

"It means shy." He laughed, and in response Penelope managed a tight smile. "My sister's name is Catriona—we call her Cat. We all love her, and she gets away with all manner of naughtiness."

She noticed when he spoke of his family, he was more relaxed, and his Scots accent was more prominent. "Your family are close?"

"Aye, verra close."

Penelope often asked herself whether it was acceptable to be jealous of other people's families. She and Mortimer were close, or they had been once upon a time, but it would be nice to have more siblings, or even to have her parents back. She missed what she might have had if that coach had not overturned when it did and taken them from her. It was like an ache in her chest that never really went away.

When she looked up, she found he was watching her reflectively, as if he was trying to read her thoughts. Quickly, she shuttered them and called out to Selina, "Are you ready? Something slow to begin with until we see how musically inclined MacKenzie is."

"Watch your toes," Selina warned, and MacKenzie laughed in that good-natured way.

Penelope had expected him to be clumsy, and she wasn't sure why. Perhaps she just hoped he would have an unfortunate lack of timing so she could forget how much she was attracted to him and instead find fault with him. But he surprised her. He was graceful, and despite a tendency to want to swing her around far too enthusiastically, he listened to her instructions and followed them. MacKenzie could be trained, she told herself, as they moved about in the cramped area at one side of the room. Next, she would need to find a proper ballroom in which to continue his lessons, and with her tarnished reputation, that was always problematic.

As for the heat of his hand clasping hers, and the heavy weight of his other hand at her waist . . . Penelope struggled to ignore both. Yes, it made her feel hot and achy with a need she dared not give free rein while she rigidly held at bay any inappropriateness.

Until he drew her in closer, and she felt the warmth of his breath against her crown as he bent toward her, and the hard warmth of his thighs with only her skirts and his pantaloons as a barrier between them. Her heart began to thump, and her cheeks felt on fire. She was imagining erotic things again. Him lifting her up and pressing her to the wall, his hand under her clothing, between her legs, giving her the relief she so sorely needed.

It was too much.

Penelope stepped back and managed a stiff nod at Selina to finish playing.

MacKenzie looked a little confused, and when she felt able to meet his brown eyes, they seemed reproachful. "I *have* danced before." He confirmed what she had already suspected. "My mother likes to dance, and when my father is not available, she dances with her sons. Cat too. We usually perform country dances, but occasionally something more formal. Dancing is no' a problem for me, Miss Armstrong."

"Your mother is a good teacher," Penelope said, trying to sound less emotionally wrought. "All the same, dancing in a familiar setting is different to a formal dance in a ballroom with everyone watching."

"I don't mind them watching," he said lightly. "The *Ghillie Callum* is a favorite with us MacKenzies. I can do that if you like?" And he was smiling again, that hint of wickedness in the curve of his lips.

"The *Ghillie Callum?*" She stumbled over the unfamiliar words.

"The Sword Dance."

"No, thank you," she said firmly. "You can tell your aunt that I am very pleased with your dancing thus far. If you continue to do well, it is more than likely you will be dancing at her ball in three weeks."

His expression brightened at her praise—Why was it so charming? "Are we finished then, Miss Armstrong?" He caught up his neckcloth, but instead of retying it about his throat, he pushed it into his jacket pocket.

"For now," she said in her sternest voice. "We start again tomorrow. We will go for a stroll in Hyde Park and see how you manage there."

As she gave him his instructions, he listened obediently, but she sensed he thought the stroll would be easy. However, Penelope knew that watching how the *ton* behaved in various situations was not simple at all. He would be observing gentlemen and ladies meeting and greeting and learning how to ape them. A man like Callum would probably find such insipid social interactions tedious, but they were necessary in the world he wanted to enter.

"Good day then, Miss Armstrong. Selina."

The door closed and Penelope wondered why the sitting room seemed bigger without him in it, as if there was more air for her to breathe. Surely one man could not take up so much space? She was still mulling over it when Selina came to perch beside her on the settee.

"Lord, that man! When he stripped off his clothing . . . I

wanted to climb all over him." Her eyes were sly as she observed Penelope.

"I am very glad you did not," was all she said.

Selina was not that easily silenced. "You appeared to be a little breathless yourself, miss."

"Not at all," she retorted. But she was lying, and Selina knew it.

Penelope stood up. "I am going to visit my brother. I should not be too long . . . I hope."

Selina understood this would not be a happy visit. "Sometimes," she said sympathetically, "I think you have far too many worries on your plate. A man like MacKenzie may be just what you need to take your mind off them. I can tell he is interested in you, so why not amuse yourself? How could it hurt to have a little fun for a change?"

Penelope shook her head very decidedly. "No, Selina. Under no circumstances. If I allow myself to be distracted just once and I am found out . . . I could lose all I have built up over the past three years. Polite society is very unforgiving," she added glumly.

Selina pouted—not a pleasant look on a woman of forty years—as Penelope closed the door. What she had said was nothing but the truth. If she did anything to bring her already soiled name into disrepute, she would lose all she had gained. No more clients, no more recommendations. She would be set adrift with no prospect of earning a living, and what would become of her then? What would become of Mortimer?

He relied on her and that was all very well, but she had decided that today was the day she would have to tell him there would be no more "loans" from her. She would continue to pay for his share of his lodgings as well as items like food and clothing, but he would have to learn to stand on his own two feet. He needed to find employment and stop letting Uncle Bertie encourage him with his ridiculous inventions.

She went downstairs, tying the ribbons of her bonnet under her chin. Suddenly, she felt very weary. Had Mortimer really expected her to return to being a gentleman's mistress, just so he could have more spending money? She did not want to believe he was so selfish. She hoped she was wrong. She hoped when she arrived at the lodgings he shared with Uncle Bertie, Mortimer would listen to her and understand.

But Penelope suspected it was going to be a very difficult conversation.

CHAPTER SEVEN

"ARE YOU SURE this is where we are meant to meet?" Angus was looking at Callum in a doubtful manner. The park, with its paths through lush green grass and shady trees, was hectic with strolling persons, while carriages and riders vied for space on the wider trails.

"This is it," Callum said.

Angus grunted. Callum felt like pointing out that that was not what a gentleman did in polite circles, but he doubted Angus would appreciate his helpful advice.

The older man directed his attention to a gentleman in skin-tight pantaloons, his cravat so high he could barely turn his head, and his hat perched on top of curled and primped hair. "Look at yon peacock," he said, forgetting to lower his voice.

The gentleman in question turned to stare, lifting a quizzing glass to his eyes. He took in Angus's splendor—he was wearing a kilt—and smirked before turning away again.

Until then, Callum had been pleased that Angus was here with him. There was something about the man's pithy comments and occasional deep laughter that made him feel less homesick. Now he was wondering if it had been a mistake. Especially when he had insisted on wearing his kilt as usual.

"I am what I am," he said, when Callum had tried to tell him that the people of London were not used to seeing a man in a skirt. "You should be proud to wear the MacKenzie colors. What would your father say?"

Callum struggled briefly with his doubts but eventually he had worn his kilt too. The dark green tartan was firm about his hips and swung jauntily as he walked. The cool air on his lower legs, and higher too beneath the shielding fabric, was pleasingly familiar.

And yet they were the recipients of stares and whispers, and a nursemaid walking with some children gave a little shriek and pulled her charges to safety.

Penelope was not going to like this, but he told himself any woman he chose to marry would have to get used to seeing him in his native finery.

"What a place this is!" Angus growled, sending a scathing look after the nursemaid. "I would never question your father's decision to send you south, but surely there are wives aplenty at home."

"He says we need a gentlewoman," Callum reminded him. "A well-bred lady who knows which spoon to use at the dinner table and what to say to awkward guests. The ladies at home look down upon us. And sometimes . . ." He bit his lip. "You remember when Sir Hector insisted Cook had not made the oatcakes the way they should be?"

"Aye, and your mother told him to go and cook his own," Angus said with a laugh.

"Well, a lady would not do that. She would smooth over the situation, not make it worse. Sir Hector refuses to speak to us now."

"Your mother has a temper, aye, but she is still a lady."

Callum knew that to be true, but his mother had never been very good at diplomacy. If the MacKenzies were to rise through the ranks of nobles to the top, where they belonged, then they needed someone who could navigate a way through the pitfalls.

"I'm not saying it is what I want, but my father is ambitious for his children," Callum said. "He has a vision for our future. He wants us to *give* the orders rather than bow to those who currently make them."

Angus gave him a bewildered look but was wise enough not to argue.

Callum understood his father's desire to see his children thrive in a cut-throat world, but he was not sure he shared it. He was happy with the way things were, with his quiet life at Bonnyrigg. If his wife wanted to rub shoulders with titled gentlemen and ladies, she could, and good luck to her, but he preferred to spend his days away from such distracting noise.

A horseman rode by, and Callum looked after him longingly, thinking of Midnight, but Penelope had specified they were to be on foot. Perhaps she did not trust him. Perhaps she thought he might gallop at full speed through the park and frighten everyone. Callum was not a fool, he understood he couldn't do that, but he needed to be patient with her until she declared him ready for Aunt Jennie's ball.

His aunt had spoken to him this morning over breakfast. "I think I would like to hear from Miss Armstrong herself when you are ready for the ball. It will give me a chance to discuss your progress, and I am curious to meet her."

Callum had shrugged. "I think I am progressing very well. Walking in the park can't be that hard, can it, Aunt?"

Jennie had paused with her coffee cup halfway to her lips. "I don't know, Callum. But I remember your father in his kilt on his wedding day. No one had ever seen the like."

Callum smiled. He imagined Maxwell on that day, marrying the duke's daughter in all her finery. And they were still together, still in love, and he did not doubt they would remain so. If he could find someone like that, he would have made his father happy, and himself too.

And yet whenever he thought of that faceless bride, he pictured Penelope on his arm, smiling up at him. Perhaps she had cast a spell on him after all.

He was relieved when Angus interrupted his thoughts. "I don't understand why they are all staring," he muttered. "We are wearing clothes, aren't we? We've combed our hair and washed our faces?"

"Perhaps they've heard about my attack on the boar," Callum said with a grimace.

"Aye, mabbe." Angus grimaced too. "Don't worry, the memory will fade soon enough, if you don't do anything else to get tongues clacking."

"I have already said I won't. I was sloshed. I drank that whisky to give me courage, and I went too far. If I could do it over again . . ." He hmphed.

Angus made a noise of his own but thankfully said no more.

They strolled on for a little, and then Angus said suddenly, again his voice far too loud, "Is that them? Coming toward us now? The wee lady in the pale blue gown and the muckle one in green?"

Callum looked up. The two women approaching were indeed Penelope and Selina. He was more concerned with the former, noting her fair hair fashioned in ringlets that peeped out from under her bonnet and danced about her lovely face, while her silver eyes were narrowed against the sun. Or perhaps . . . were they narrowed because there was something about *him* she disapproved of?

He admitted he wanted Penelope to approve of him, but at the same time he enjoyed unsettling her. She was so calm and composed that he longed to cause her eyes to narrow as they were now, or even to flash. He wanted to dig beneath her unruffled exterior and reveal the real woman he knew was hiding there. He wanted to see her smile as she had yesterday.

As for what else Callum wanted to do to her . . . well, they were the sort of ungentlemanly thoughts he should not be having right now.

When the two parties met, Penelope held out her hand to Callum. "My lord Marquess," she said, and gave a little curtsy.

Callum bowed. "Miss Armstrong. What a surprise! What are you doing here this fine day?"

She blinked. Her gaze dropped to his kilt and he waited for

some pithy comment, but instead she said, "Shall we go for a stroll? Please, will you join Selina and me?"

"With pleasure." He turned to Angus, who was observing them with amusement. "Angus? Will you stroll with us?"

Penelope arched a fair eyebrow. "You have not introduced us to your companion, MacKenzie. Who is this fellow?"

Damn, she was good! "This is Angus Grant, my manservant, bodyguard, and friend. Angus, this is Miss Penelope Armstrong, and Miss Selina . . .?"

"Halliday," Selina said, with a glance at Penelope. "I am Miss Armstrong's maid, and although I would like to claim I am her bodyguard, I'm not sure what that entails."

"You are my friend, too," Penelope said quickly. "And I don't think I need a bodyguard."

"You never know," Angus replied, with a wink at Selina. He gave a bow to them both. "Miss Armstrong. Miss Halliday."

"Mr. Grant," Penelope replied serenely.

Selina said nothing, seemingly fascinated by Angus's legs. Callum could see that they were particularly hairy but surely not so different from anybody else's. Hadn't she seen a man's legs before? But then he remembered how she had seemed fascinated by his bare chest and thought that perhaps she had not.

The formalities over, the four of them set out for their stroll, Callum and Penelope in the lead, and Angus and Selina following behind.

Callum tucked Penelope's gloved hand into his elbow, and she didn't demure. He also made sure to shorten his steps to match hers, ignoring the rude stares they were garnering. These were the sort of courtesies he would have shown back home at Bonnyrigg, and nothing to do with learning to be a gentleman. Perhaps he wasn't such a brute after all.

"Is your family close by?" he said, thinking of his own. He couldn't imagine not living near to his own family.

"No." She gave him a sideways glance as if judging whether to share a confidence with him. Callum waited, hoping she would trust him. When she spoke, her voice was cool and matter-of-fact. "I am an orphan, MacKenzie. My parents were killed in a coach accident just over ten years ago."

That shocked him. He tried to imagine it, his parents gone in a moment and him left alone in the world. The Scottish slang word slipped from his lips before he could stop it. "Jings!"

"I hope that wasn't profane," she said gravely, but her lips twitched as she restrained a smile.

"No, no, I was just surprised," he assured her, recovering himself. "And you have no one else? No other family?"

"My brother, and I have an uncle." Her expression altered slightly, and he thought that fact did not give her pleasure. Secrets. Penelope had secrets, and Callum wanted to know what they were. But he understood that quizzing people, unless you knew them very well, was impolite.

"Were you in the coach with your parents?" he asked instead, bending his head to listen to her reply. The feather in her bonnet tickled his nose and he tried not to sneeze.

"No. They were visiting friends, and my brother and I were at home. Mortimer was eight years old, so I took over his care."

Her voice wobbled a little, and suddenly he longed to wrap his arms about her and hold her fast. To comfort her. But she recovered herself quickly, and he knew better than to persist with questions that she found distressing.

"Perhaps we should speak about your stay in London," she said briskly in her teaching voice. "I want you to wax lyrical about the sights, MacKenzie. Pretend I am a possible wife and impress me."

Callum smiled, but the trouble was he did not have to pretend. He wasn't such a fool as to tell her so, but knowing how he felt confused him and worried him a little.

Wax lyrical . . .?

He did his best. As yet, he had not seen many of the popular sights, but he spoke of the ones he would *like* to see. He was in the middle of a possible visit to the Tower of London, when a shout interrupted him.

"Damn it," Penelope murmured irritably.

Selina, who had been trailing behind with Angus, came to stand beside her to form a battle line. "What is he doing here?" she said. Then, "He doesn't look happy."

Penelope's fingers tightened on Callum's arm and he covered her hand with his. Her gaze was fixed on the young man who was approaching them. A portly older gentleman was some steps behind, red-faced as he hurried to keep up with his companion.

"You are about to meet my brother Mortimer," Penelope said reluctantly. "And my Uncle Bertie."

Callum could see the resemblance between the younger man and his sister—they both had the same fair hair and slight stature—although Mortimer's face wore an angry scowl. Bertie was in a checked coat, and his grey hair looked as if it had been caught in a gale. His cravat was crooked and his boots too big. Compared to Mortimer's neat outfit, Bertie could have dressed in the dark.

Was that how some people thought of him? He could comfort himself that at least today he was well turned out.

Without greeting his sister, Mortimer burst into furious recriminations. "Did you really think we would leave things as they were yesterday? If you refuse to help, then how can Uncle Bertie and I carry on with our work? We are at a crucial point! Surely you can see how selfish you are being, Pen?"

"Mortimer," Penelope sounded weary. She glanced about her and lowered her voice. "I beg you will not do this here. We can speak later." She glanced up at Callum. "At the moment, I have a guest with me."

Mortimer seemed to see Callum for the first time. Angus glared at the boy, attempting to intimidate him, and Callum gave him a warning nudge with his elbow.

"Good God, are you taking on barbarians as clients now?" Mortimer burst out, and then he gave a sneering sort of snigger.

Callum wondered whether he was hearing things. Apart from

the insult to himself, he knew if *he* spoke to his sister like that, she would hit him over the head with one of the medieval shields that hung in the banqueting hall at Bonnyrigg. And he would deserve it.

"Are you casting aspersions on the Marquess of Morven, you wee numbskull?" Angus growled at his side, sounding like a dog about to slip its leash.

Mortimer seemed to hesitate, as well he might, then chose to ignore Angus and turned back to his sister.

"Uncle Bertie and I need to finish our work. What are we supposed to do now?" He sighed as if the world was against him. "I do wish you would stop this nonsense, Pen. It is degrading. At least when you were with Lord Muir, we were guaranteed financial security. He looked after you! Us! I really wish you would reconsider your future before it is too late and you are too old to attract another protector."

Callum momentarily froze. He heard Selina give a gasp, and Angus another growl. Penelope had lost all the color from her face, and when she finally answered, her voice was low and shaky.

"Enough, Mortimer. I said what I had to say yesterday. I cannot help you any further with your ridiculous schemes and you should not ask it of me. As for the rest . . . if I thought you meant what you said, offering me to the highest bidder, I would no longer want you for my brother."

In contrast to his sister, Mortimer's face flushed red. With embarrassment or rage? Callum thought it might be a combination of both. "I am only speaking the truth. Everything was so much better before you decided to pretend to be respectable. No one cares, Pen! You will never be invited back to those proper houses, and why would you want to be? Boring dinner parties and balls with boring people!"

"You don't know what you're talking about," she began, and Callum could feel her shaking through the hand that still grasped his arm.

This appalling scene had to stop. He could see they had attracted a great deal of attention already. "Go away," he said, seething but still trying to be the polite gentleman Penelope wanted him to be. "You have said more than enough, you wee gowk."

Mortimer shot him a savage look, although Callum suspected his bravery was a façade to hide his fear. "Let her go, you damned brute!" he said with gritted teeth and tried to release Penelope's hand from Callum's arm. "Leave my sister alone!"

It was too much.

Callum struck the boy square on his chin and Mortimer went down.

CHAPTER EIGHT

THERE WAS A moment of utter silence. "I say," Uncle Bertie gasped. "Hardly a gentlemanly thing to do." He seemed to be considering some sort of retaliation, until he caught Callum's eye and Angus stepped forward. Choosing to retreat, Bertie went to Mortimer's aid. The boy was already trying to get up and shook off his uncle, holding a hand to his chin. His eyes were shiny with tears, but whether of pain, rage, or embarrassment, again Callum wasn't sure.

The crowd around them had increased in size. There were excited gasps and shocked faces.

"I think we should leave now," Angus murmured, "before we are arrested."

Callum didn't need the warning. He should be annoyed with himself for having undone all of his good work since the boar incident, but he could not feel sorry. The way Mortimer had spoken to his sister . . . His behavior had been utterly contemptible. Callum didn't care what he had called Angus and himself, but to insult Penelope like that, to suggest she would be better off becoming some man's mistress just so that her brother had enough spending money to do whatever it was he did . . . No, Callum could not ignore that.

Mortimer was allowing his uncle to lead him away, although every now and again he would turn and shoot back a furious glance at his sister.

"Spoiled young pup," Angus muttered. He shook his head at

Callum. "And I should tell you off for making yourself notorious again, but I canna find it in my heart. You did the right thing there, lad."

Callum thought so too, but he wasn't sure Penelope would agree.

Selina had her arm about her friend, subtly holding her up, and Penelope took a deep breath and said, "I am so sorry. This is not at all what I had hoped for from today." She still sounded very shaken. Callum was concerned to see how little of her usual serenity remained, and her beautiful face was still as white as a ghost, while her eyes were wide and filled with tears.

He didn't like it. He didn't like to see her like this.

He wished he had punched Mortimer twice, no matter the consequences to himself.

"Come," he said abruptly, and slipped her hand once more into the crook of his elbow. He began to lead her back the way they had come, toward the entrance to the park. "We have my aunt's carriage," he said. "She insisted. Her house is not far. I will take you there so that you can compose yourself."

She began to protest, but she sounded breathless and even a little scared. The Penelope he knew had not sounded like this before and it unsettled him even more. Now he was wondering if he could hunt Mortimer down and strangle him. Selina's eyes were big too, as if she rarely saw her mistress so disturbed, and she appeared relieved to hand over the decision of what to do to Callum.

Before long, they were aboard the carriage and on their way through the streets of Mayfair.

Penelope was staring ahead, blinking furiously to stop her tears from falling, while Selina held her hand and murmured words meant to comfort her, but which seemed to be more about what an ungrateful wretch Mortimer was.

Callum and Angus exchanged a look.

Of course Penelope was upset with her brother and uncle. Mortimer's abuse had been sickening. Did the boy even know what he was asking of her? Callum would have liked to explain it to him in detail, *while* he was strangling him. He wondered what would have happened if he had not been there to protect her. And then he wondered if Mortimer had done this before— insulted and abused her and made her cry.

Strangling was far too good for the boy.

"I shouldn't have refused him the money," Penelope said softly, and despite her efforts, a tear spilled over her lashes and rolled down her cheek. "I thought it was for his own good, but now I can see I have destroyed whatever was left between us. He will never forgive me. I have lost my brother forever."

"About time you refused," Selina retorted. "He is bleeding you dry. It cannot go on. You needed to tell him. I just wish he had not taken it so badly."

"But he is all I have," Penelope wailed. She bit her lip, but it would not stop trembling. "And now I have no one."

Callum could bear it no longer.

He reached forward and took her free hand in his. She looked up in surprise, as if she had forgotten he was there, and he met her eyes and held her gaze. "Listen to me, Miss Armstrong. That is not the way a brother treats his sister. I have a sister, and I would never speak like that to her—she would not allow me to even if I were foolish enough to try. Your brother needs to learn he cannot act like a spoiled child to get his own way."

Another tear ran down her cheek.

Callum groaned. He wanted nothing more than to take her in his arms. He ached with the desire to comfort her, but he restrained himself. He doubted she would allow it, and if he tried, it would probably only make things worse.

When they reached Aunt Jennie's townhouse, the horrible Hocking opened the door to them. Confronted by four people, two of them Scottish barbarians, his usually immobile face didn't seem to know what to do with itself.

"Do you have an appointment?" he said, blocking the door- way.

"Out of the way, Hocking," Callum replied, pushing by. "Where is my aunt?"

"She has guests. My lord." The title seemed to injure his dignity as he spoke it. "I do not advise you join her right now." He was staring at Penelope in horror. Obviously he recognized her, and Callum might have punched him, too, if Penelope had not intervened.

"Oh no, no," she said. "I do not want to be a spectacle."

"Where is Aunt Jennie?" Callum asked Hocking again.

"The countess is in the drawing room." Hocking seemed to think that was obvious.

Callum took Penelope's hand firmly in his and led her toward the parlor, calling over his shoulder to the butler, "Tea, Hocking, and be quick about it."

Angus chuckled once the door was closed and they were alone. "You will give that man an apoplexy."

"An apoplexy is the least he deserves," Callum said. He was watching Penelope. She was stripping off her gloves and then untying her bonnet, but her actions seemed stiff and automatic, her mind far away. Whatever Selina was whispering to her was ignored, as she sat down on the couch.

Making another decision, he opened the door again and shouted. "Whisky, Hocking."

Selina looked about to burst with excitement, but she had the presence of mind to inform them that, "Miss Armstrong does not drink whisky. She prefers brandy."

Callum nodded and shouted again. "Make that brandy, Hocking."

Shortly afterward, Hocking arrived with a brandy decanter and a small glass upon an ornate silver tray. He set it down with elaborate care, before bowing stiffly and closing the door quietly behind him.

Angus snorted, and Selina giggled nervously. Callum poured a small amount of the liquid into a glass and took Selina's place beside Penelope. He put the glass into her hand and when she didn't seem to notice it, lifted it to her lips. She drank and then coughed, but drank again, on her own this time. Then she leaned back and closed her eyes.

"Does this happen often?" Callum asked, not taking his gaze off Penelope.

"Not often. Not as often as it used to," Selina said reluctantly. "And when it does, it is usually because of some upset caused by her brother. She just needs a moment to—to gather herself."

Everyone watched, holding their breath. When Penelope's eyes opened, Callum was glad to see they were more alert, and she looked about her with surprise, followed by resignation. "Oh," she said with weary sarcasm, "it wasn't a nightmare then."

Callum smiled with relief and said, "And there you are, my bonny lass."

CHAPTER NINE

PENELOPE WONDERED HOW long she had been absent. Taken back in her memory to those dark days after her parents died. It didn't happen as often as it used to, but when it did, it could be frightening. For her as well as for those around her. She was a woman who knew her own mind, as well as being brave and forthright, and she had no trouble standing up for herself, but when Mortimer was upset with her, she fell to pieces.

It was embarrassing and infuriating, but she couldn't seem to help it. She felt as if she was back in the past, when the coach had tipped over and her parents had died, and she had found herself alone and solely responsible for her young brother. The realization that she was all he had had been terrifying.

Now she wondered, had she failed him? Surely not. She had done everything in her power to protect and care for him, but when the moment had finally come for her to follow her own dreams and desires, she had taken it. And Mortimer had not gone without. She had scraped together the funds he needed, often going without herself, and yet he was still not satisfied. Where had the sweet little boy gone, the one who had gazed up at her as if she were the moon and the stars to him?

The bond between them had been broken. Perhaps irreparably.

Today, her brother's fury at her, the cruel and hurtful things he had said, had once again caused her to crumble. That was bad enough, but Callum had seen her feebleness. How was she to regain her authority as his tutor? And that wasn't the worst of it. People in the park had been watching, ladies and gentlemen and common folk, all of them reveling in her downfall. They probably believed it was just what a woman like her deserved—How dare she try to claw her way back to respectability? And now they would all be gossiping.

She had worked so hard to put her past behind her, and although it could never be entirely forgotten, she had made some great strides. Now, through one awful moment, she had lost that hard won ground and was back where she started.

Well, it was done now. She must deal with it.

Stiffening her spine, she met Callum MacKenzie's brown eyes. What was she going to see in them? Pity? Disgust? After she had accepted Lord Muir's proposal, she had read both in the gaze of people she had thought her friends. But to her surprise, Callum's were warm with concern, and she felt the turmoil inside her settle a little. Mortimer had decided his needs and wants were more important than hers, and Uncle Bertie only cared for her when she could continue to supply him with funds for his inventions. And yet here was a man she barely knew, looking at her like he was prepared to do anything to make the situation better.

It made her feel confused, rather dizzy, and *happy*. A great torrent of happiness such as she had not felt in such a long while swept through her. A warm rush of *gladness* that he was here at her side.

And—she sat up straighter—it was quite, quite wrong!

Callum was her client, and she never allowed intimacies with her clients. No matter how attractive he was, and how much she wanted right now for him to lean down and capture her lips with his. How she longed to tuck herself into his arms and hold on. It could not happen.

Besides, he was frowning now. He was probably wondering why she was staring at him so foolishly. Penelope took in a deep breath while she tried to regain her equilibrium.

Remember who you are. Remember how much is riding on your business with this man. Even if, after today, you never receive another client request, you can still make Callum MacKenzie the best that he can possibly be. Surely that is a goal to aim for?

She found her voice. "I apologize for my brother. He has made us the subject of gossip, and I have no doubt the tale will soon be everywhere. That is not helpful to either one of us. But I am willing to press on with your lessons, if you are happy to allow me to do so. Perhaps we can start afresh tomorrow, MacKenzie?"

He looked thoughtful, and then, to her relief, he nodded briskly. "I am happy with our arrangement. And as I am already the subject of gossip, a wee bit more hardly matters. Tomorrow it is then, Miss Armstrong."

Relieved, she managed a smile, which he returned. He really was such a handsome man, and that observation was *not* helpful.

Penelope stood up and looked around her at the room. Where was she again? Oh yes, the Countess of Strathmore's London home. Selina had risen too, taking her lead from Penelope and preparing to leave, but she looked concerned.

"Are you sure you are well enough?" she said quietly, and then seemed to think better of it when Penelope shot her a warning look. "Of course you are!" She gave a nervous laugh. "What am I thinking? Everything is excellent."

At that moment, a woman Penelope assumed to be the Countess of Strathmore opened the door and then stood staring at them all in amazement. "Hocking said there was a plague of persons in here, but I thought he was joking! Callum, explain yourself."

"Hocking made a joke?" Callum asked with pretended incredulity. Then, seeing she was not amused, hurried on. "I apologize, Aunt Jennie, but as you know, we were at the park, and Miss Armstrong was indisposed. I knew you would not mind if I brought her here to recover. Which she has."

The two of them exchanged a look, and then the countess

gave Callum the sort of smile that always made Penelope's heart ache. A loving smile, an understanding smile, the smile of a parent to a child—or in this case, an aunt to a nephew. A smile she would never receive again in her life.

"Miss Armstrong," the countess spoke warmly, "despite the circumstances of your visit, I am glad you are here. Do tell me how my nephew's lessons are progressing. Have you pulled him into ship shape, as my husband would say?"

Penelope was still shaken, but this was not the time to appear weak. She wrapped her famed serenity around her inner disquiet and answered confidently.

"The marquess will be in ship shape very soon. A few more lessons and he will be ready to appear at your ball in his honor. I am sure there will be ladies aplenty eager for his addresses."

The countess looked pleased. "That is good to hear!" She hesitated and then went on with a frown. "However, that being said . . . it is my brother-in-law who wants him to find a virtuous and well-connected wife; I'd prefer he found one who made him happy."

She spoke bluntly, and Callum looked embarrassed at being discussed so intimately.

"Surely both are possible?" Penelope said. "I know that it is rare to fall in love with one's spouse, but it is not beyond the realm of probability."

The countess's lips twitched in amusement. "Indeed. My own marriage was a love match. And Callum's parents are still disgustingly in love despite four children. I think it very unfair of them to ask their son to marry for anything other than love."

Did she really believe that? If so, Penelope wondered what on earth the MacKenzies were thinking to send their son down to London on a quest for a wife. Although the dream of being with someone you loved was a pleasant one, it was extremely unlikely. Penelope could not hope for such an ending. And even if it were possible, who on earth would offer for her, in the circumstances?

Besides, did she really want to fall in love and place her future in the hands of one man? She had already known the highs and lows of life as a gentleman's property, and that had left her determined to keep her independence and make her own way in the world. Had one glimpse of Callum's smile and his warm, brown eyes turned everything she had learned in the past ten years on its head?

Of course not!

And she reminded herself that even if by some unlikely chance Callum did set his sights on her, why would he feel the need to propose? Marquesses did not marry women who were damaged goods. Probably after one illicit night in her arms, in her bed, he would move on to his real objective—a suitable wife. And she would be left behind.

The countess was watching her with speculative, grey eyes and Penelope realized she had allowed the silence to go on for far too long. She pulled herself together and desperately hoped her face had not betrayed her ridiculous thoughts.

"Tomorrow we will resume our lessons in—in conversation," she said, plucking a subject out of the air. She looked about and, seeing her bonnet and gloves, gathered them up. "And I will arrange for your nephew to attend a ball, to ensure his conduct is flawless."

"Well, that sounds most satisfactory," the countess said, clapping her hands. She glanced behind her, where Hocking was hovering outside the door. "Do excuse me, Miss Armstrong. My guests will be wondering where I am. Perhaps we will meet again?"

Penelope smiled and curtsied.

"And, my dear, I insist you take the carriage home. No, I will not take no for an answer!" And she was gone in a swirl of silk and perfume.

Penelope had found the countess polite and friendly, quite unlike most of the titled ladies she had previously come face to face with. It made her feel almost hopeful, until she remembered the scene in the park. Once the countess heard about that, she would almost certainly remove her nephew from such contagion.

Selina touched her hand and lifted an enquiring brow.

Penelope snapped herself out of her unhappy thoughts. "I will see you tomorrow," she said, turning to Callum.

He was watching her somberly. She suspected he was going to ask if she needed his assistance with her brother, and she could not have that. She gave him a little curtsy and left the room.

The butler, Hocking, his nose in the air, opened the door for her and then shut it quickly.

"Well, that was awkward," Selina said quietly at her side. "What are you going to do?"

"Resist," Penelope said. "I am going to harden myself against him. Anything else is impossible."

Selina seemed to be trying not to smile. "I meant what are you going to do about Mortimer, but it is good to know you are going to resist MacKenzie. I'm not sure I could."

Realizing her mistake, Penelope avoided her maid's eyes and said hurriedly, "It was unpleasant, yes. I am sure the gossips are spreading the news as we speak, but there is nothing I can do about it. Mortimer never thinks before he acts. In many ways, he is still a child. I am going to stand firm, even though I know we will be at odds for . . . I am sorry for it, but . . ." She swallowed, grief a lump in her throat.

"Thank goodness," Selina retorted. "It is about time. You are doing the right thing."

Penelope tried to smile but couldn't quite manage it. Mortimer might never forgive her or understand why she had refused him when before she had always given in to his demands. In most ways, she was a strong and capable woman, but he was her one weakness. Was she to blame?

"You mentioned a ball?" Selina said.

Penelope gratefully jumped at the distraction. "Yes, I thought the Livingstones' ball next week."

Selina grinned. "You mean the Bohemian Ball?"

"Well, yes. It isn't like I will be invited to Almack's," she retorted sharply. "And it doesn't matter if it isn't quite the thing. All MacKenzie requires is to dance and make conversation, just as he would at any ball. And I will see he does not get into any trouble."

"They will seize upon him like starving cats," was Selina's delighted response.

Penelope did not answer. She would make sure nothing happened to Callum MacKenzie, and she would deliver him safely home to his aunt.

"You should wear your rose-pink gown," Selina said with a glint in her eyes. "It suits you so well, and you never wear it these days."

"Where would I go in it?" Penelope spoke lightly. "And this ball is not about me, Selina, as you well know."

Selina hummed an answer, but Penelope wasn't convinced. Her friend was up to mischief, and she suspected it had something to do with Callum MacKenzie.

"Before the ball, I will need to address MacKenzie's choice of clothing," she said thoughtfully. "Make an appointment with Doddington as soon as possible."

Doddington had been Lord Muir's tailor, and they had remained friends. Penelope used him for her clients whenever necessary, and he sent his customers to her if he thought they needed her help.

Penelope only hoped Callum was still her client after his aunt heard about Mortimer and the park.

CHAPTER TEN

CALLUM ARRIVED THE next morning for his lessons. The art of polite conversation was something he felt he had already mastered. Yes, it was useful to know what he should say to who and when, but the trouble was when he was speaking to Penelope, he wasn't really concentrating on what he was saying.

After the "wee brawl in the park," as Angus was calling it, he had seen just how vulnerable Penelope was. Not that he thought of her as weak, but he could see she was struggling with her brother's selfish behavior and was letting her fear of losing him interfere with the need to be firm with him. He supposed if he had lost his parents and brought up his brother on his own, then he might struggle to draw boundaries, too.

Mortimer hadn't been mentioned again, so he couldn't offer her his advice, even if she wanted it. However, the tale of the brawl had been spread near and wide, and the report of his confrontation with the boy had taken on a life of its own. He was a "base beast" and shouldn't be allowed out in public. His aunt had come to him later, wide-eyed and worried, and asked what on earth had happened at the park before he brought Miss Armstrong to her house.

Callum had told her as clearly and emotionlessly as he could, saying he had stepped in when the boy had crossed a line. After Jennie heard what had been said to Penelope, she had seemed conflicted. "I can see why you felt you had to stand up for Miss Armstrong. You were always a considerate boy, Callum, but I think you could have done so without violence. Now you have embroiled yourself in another scandal."

"I'm sorry." He had sighed. "It just made me so angry. She is trying . . . I believe she is trying her best to give him everything he asks for, but he doesn't appreciate her efforts. He only sees the situation from his point of view. If I dared to speak like that to Cat—"

"You wouldn't," Jennie had said with certainty. "You're a good lad, Callum, with your heart in the right place, but you need to be careful. I am not sure your parents would want you to continue with these lessons, but I see the improvement in you so I am going to suggest you carry on. But as far as possible, you must distance yourself from Miss Armstrong. I know that might be tricky, but you are clever enough not to allow your feelings about her situation with her brother to be engaged. She could seriously damage you. I admire her for what she has done with her life. It would have been so much easier for her to find another protector and carry on as before, but she didn't take that road. She struck out on her own. I admire her for that and would like to support her efforts, but not at your expense."

Jennie had taken a breath before continuing. "Now, as for the gossips, we need to show them we are not concerned with their nasty stories. I have always thought that the way to do that is to ignore them and carry on with our plans. Something else will capture their interest—it always does. But having said that . . . Callum, you really do need to be careful where Miss Armstrong is concerned."

"I know. I will. And thank you," Callum had said humbly. He was grateful for his aunt's understanding and would try to keep his distance, but the truth was it was becoming increasingly difficult to do so.

When he was with Penelope, he wanted to kiss her. He wanted to hold her in his arms. He wanted far too many things he knew he could not have, but the awkward thing was, sometimes when he saw her looking at him, he wondered if she wanted those same things.

"You seem distracted," Penelope said now.

Startled from his thoughts, Callum gave her a guilty look. "I was far away. I'm sorry. You were telling me what I should say to an earl as opposed to a baron . . .?"

Penelope glanced at the ticking clock on the mantelpiece. "It doesn't matter. You have an appointment. We are going to see Mr. Doddington."

"And who is Mr. Doddington?" he asked with a frown, and couldn't help but wonder if this was some new form of torture.

"He is a tailor, and the best in London. He has helped me before with those of my clients who lacked fashion sense."

Callum looked down at his baggy breeches. "I can't see the point in you fitting me out like a dandy when I will be returning to the forests of Bonnyrigg. I doubt the squirrels and the deer will care what I am wearing."

"Well, there *is* a point, MacKenzie," she said severely, and he felt that familiar clench in his stomach.

He cleared his throat. "I am not arguing. I know I will need formal evening wear for Aunt Jennie's ball. She mentioned it the other day."

"Good. We will save her the trouble, and I know Mr. Doddington will have you looking just the thing in no time."

Callum couldn't think of anything more boring than being fitted for clothing he would never wear again. Standing about while his size and his measurements were discussed. But he could see that Penelope was adamant.

"Very well," he said. "Your wish is my command."

At that moment, Selina tapped on the door. After conferring in whispers, Penelope excused herself, and Callum was left to kick his heels. He couldn't help but wonder if Mortimer was giving his sister more grief, but he reminded himself it was none of his business. His aunt's warning was fresh in his mind and he must ignore his instincts when it came to protecting Penelope Armstrong.

He was not her knight in shining armor and he could not save her. She was not for him.

Then why did he feel as if she was?

"I'M SORRY TO be the bearer of bad news," Selina said in a low voice. "Mrs. Parker is waiting to speak to you. And I received this while you were with MacKenzie."

She held out a note with an impressive looking seal. Penelope recognized it as belonging to one of her upcoming clients, or at least the mother of that client.

She broke the seal. The note was brief and said exactly what she had expected. Her services were no longer required. No explanation, but then none was needed. The incident with Mortimer in the park had done its damage.

Penelope took a deep breath and told herself she could still repair the mess she found herself in. All she needed to do was turn Callum from a "barbarian" into a gentleman, find him a suitable wife, and then receive the congratulations she rightly deserved for performing such a miracle. Surely then everyone would see she was worthy of another chance?

"Bad news?" Selina was watching her face, her own expression sympathetic. "You always said that woman was a stickler. I hope her son is snubbed by the *ton*."

Penelope managed a smile. "He should be with that silly laugh of his. Although almost anything is forgiven when one has a title and a fortune."

Selina hesitated. "Do you think Mrs. Parker—"

"Is here to tell me she no longer requires my services for her granddaughter? Probably. I had better speak to her."

Mrs. Parker, with her beaky nose, had the appearance of a bird of ill omen. She explained in a breathless voice that although she would be happy for Penelope to take on her granddaughter for her next, and *fifth*, Season with no husband in sight, her family were not.

"I fear you have turned a great many supporters against you, Miss Armstrong," she said. "Such a to-do with your brother and that brute, MacKenzie. What next? No one wants to risk employing you in case their reputations are tarnished by association."

It was nothing more than Penelope had expected, but it still hurt. She forced herself to say, "I understand, Mrs. Parker, and I apologize. Perhaps at some point in the future, if you need my services again—"

Mrs. Parker waved a hand to stop her. "The thing is," she said, her voice shaking, "I know you could have helped my poor granddaughter find her feet this Season. She struggles so with shyness. I have seen the change you have made in so many others. I just wish . . ."

But whatever she wished was not spoken, and Mrs. Parker left soon afterward.

Penelope stood for a time, contemplating the future that lay before her, but it was too gloomy for her to do so for long. Besides, she still had one client, and he was waiting for her upstairs. She wouldn't let this stop her from turning Callum into her greatest triumph. She would show them all!

CHAPTER ELEVEN

MR. DODDINGTON WAS a tall, spare man with sharp eyes behind his round spectacles. He always had a smile for Penelope, and now he listened as she introduced him to Callum and explained what was required for her latest client. "I think he needs a complete transformation."

Callum made a sound that suggested he disagreed.

"Hmm." Doddington gave Callum a searching examination. "The marquess certainly has the right figure for the latest fashions."

"I'm not a dandy," Callum muttered.

Doddington's mouth twitched. "No, you are *not* a dandy," he agreed, "but you could be much admired if you put your mind to it, my lord. I see you in clothing that fits you without a wrinkle. Plain colors—none of those silly sparkly waistcoats. You would be the envy of the *ton*, and that is the point, isn't it, Miss Armstrong?"

"That is the point," she agreed with a smile. "The marquess has come to London in search of a wife."

Doddington clapped his hands. "I think with a little help from myself and Miss Armstrong, you will find one," he said. "Now, let us get started."

Penelope was more than happy to leave matters in the tailor's hands, but she felt she had to stay in case there was a question of taste or style she needed to address. Or if Callum refused to cooperate. To pass the time, she wandered about the premises, stopping to inspect some of the rolls of cloth on display and a tub of fancy buttons. Now and again there was a murmur of voices from the inner room, but so far it sounded as if all was well.

"Miss Armstrong?" Eventually, Doddington's call brought her to the door of the fitting room. "I wonder if you could give us your thoughts on a matter of color."

Penelope blinked. Callum was standing there bare chested, in his drawers, and looking most uncomfortable. It was certainly a sight to see, but she kept her gaze on his face.

"I believe the forest green for the jacket, what do you think?" Doddington asked, seeming not to notice her discomfort or Callum's. "We could make that royal blue, but the marquess informs me he likes nothing better than to stroll in the forest on his estate. I thought the green may remind him of home."

Callum gave her a pleading look but Penelope ignored him.

"Yes, I agree," she went on. "But I also think we need more than one jacket. The marquess will be very busy socially in the next few weeks, and he can afford your excellent craftsmanship." She raised her eyebrow at Callum and caught the flicker of a smile in his dark gaze.

"Miss Armstrong knows best," he said gloomily.

The matter dealt with, she should have then left the room, and yet she lingered. Her treacherous gaze refused to be checked. And good God, the man was well built. Curved muscles in his arms and shoulders, and then there was the breadth of his chest. His thighs were also strongly built—all that striding around his estate, she supposed—and she experienced a wave of dizziness as she contemplated how he would look if he were completely naked. The bulge beneath his drawers certainly hinted at something sizeable there.

Shocked, she came to her senses, and her gaze shot upward.

Amused brown eyes were observing her. She could not pretend she had not been openly ogling him, but Penelope did her best.

"The inexpressibles would suit him too, Mr. Doddington."

"Indeed they would," Doddington agreed as he carried on with his measurements.

"*Inexpressibles?*" Callum repeated with a frown.

"They are pantaloons, sir," Doddington explained. "Very *tight* pantaloons. They do not suit everyone, although unfortunately some persons ignore the advice of their tailor and wear them anyway, but they would certainly suit you."

He thought a moment and then shrugged. "As long as I can walk in them," he decided.

Penelope felt her heart give a little jolt. He was such a *good-natured* man. He might complain a little, and sometimes sigh as if he was being put upon, but he had never outright refused to do as she told him. Well, not for long. If only there were some way . . .

But it was no use dreaming of the impossible, was it? She was being paid to make him palatable to the ladies of London—a veritable feast! Not to have him for herself.

Doddington and Penelope conferred, and he assured her that the garments they required would be finished in good time. In fact, he would get his team started immediately. "We cannot have the marquess looking anything other than the gentleman he is," he said, beaming at them both. "My reputation is at stake."

As was hers.

"Thank you, Mr. Doddington," Penelope said, and it was heartfelt. "I can always rely on you."

With Callum clothed once again, they retraced their steps to the street, where numerous shoppers lingered outside enticing establishments. Penelope couldn't help but notice the interest she and Callum attracted, but she ignored the glances and whispers as best she could. Callum appeared a little flustered, tugging at his ill-fitting jacket like he had only just realized how unflattering it was on him.

That was a good lesson, she told herself. Someone in his position needed to understand the importance of appearance. And yet at the same time she felt a twinge of regret—there had been something touching about the naivety of the man who had first come to her for help. She was not a devotee of peacocks who had to check their appearance in every shiny surface.

Lord Muir had been one such. Despite his years, he had been excessively proud of his looks, and Penelope had found it secretly amusing. The way he had to stop at every mirror he came to or examine his features in a silver dessert spoon before eating. Callum MacKenzie did not seem at all self-obsessed. He was certainly confident, most of the time anyway. She understood he must feel out of place here in London, but she imagined that when he was in familiar surroundings, he would be very much at ease.

"Your evening wear will be ready in time for the practice ball," she declared, suddenly aware of the silence stretching between them.

He nodded. Ahead of them stood a line of hackneys, and she lifted her hand to summon one. Callum hurried to open the door for her before settling in beside her.

Two ladies who were passing paused with avid gazes and whispered together behind their gloved hands. Penelope sighed and reminded herself again that while there was nothing she could do about the gossips, she could still help Callum to reach his goal. Of that she was more determined than ever, and bedamned to all those who wished her ill.

She turned to make some inconsequential comment about the weather and found him watching her. There was a question in his eyes and a quirk to his brows. "You seem distracted, Miss Armstrong," he said quietly. "Is your brother causing you more distress?"

It was a personal question, and Penelope really should remind him that personal questions should be reserved for those one knew intimately.

"Not since you knocked him down," she heard herself say drolly.

He grimaced. "Apologies. It was impulsive, and—and excessive, but I couldn't help myself."

She hesitated and then nodded. "He was rude. Although perhaps a sharp warning might have been a better choice than physical violence."

"What if I had challenged him to a duel?"

She laughed. "Mortimer would have refused. He is no expert when it comes to pistol or sword." Then, in an attempt to move on to less fraught subjects, "What of you, MacKenzie? Are you proficient in either?"

"In my own rough way, I am considered an expert shot," he said with a grin. "The sword . . ." He paused. "I do not play with that weapon—it is for serious battle. I know there are gentlemen who believe it is a game, but not me. I would only pick up a sword if it was to protect my family, my home, or my country."

He was a proud man. Penelope asked herself when the last time was that she had believed in something as strongly. Her sole reason for living seemed to be to protect Mortimer and make enough money to keep food on the table. What did the future hold for her? She had longed to escape the life of a kept woman, and so she had, but her current situation was tenuous at best. No clients were booked for future lessons, and once Callum was gone, she faced a bleak future.

The awful thing was that she was beginning to wonder if Mortimer was right. Perhaps she should seek out a new protector before it was too late. But living that life again, beholden to a man who might finish with her from one day to the next . . . The idea made her feel quite ill.

"You are lost in thought again," said a deep voice in her ear. "And your expression suggests they are not pleasant thoughts."

His warm breath brought tingles to her skin. Penelope turned her head and found him very close. His light-brown eyes were flecked with a darker color, and as she gazed into them, she admitted to herself that she found him very attractive. Almost irresistibly so.

Selina's words popped into her mind. Why not enjoy herself while she could? Was it possible for her to put aside her rules and do that? If she had no more clients and her career in tutoring was over, then what would it matter? Callum would still find his wife and return to Scotland, she would make sure of that. But right now he was here and so was she.

She wasn't sure who moved first, but she was suddenly aware of the brush of his lips on hers. Soft. Restrained. Another tingle went through her, this time accompanied by a hot wave of desire, and with a soft moan she leaned into him, her arm sliding around his neck and drawing him close.

In a heartbeat, they were kissing passionately, almost fighting for supremacy, his tongue inside her mouth and hers tangling with his. Her fingers tangled in his long hair, and his jacket buttons dug into her soft breasts. It was wondrous. So wondrous that her banked desire threatened to overwhelm any restraint she still had on it. She was lost in the moment, forgetting everything but the taste and sensation of Callum MacKenzie.

Outside the hackney, a child wailed. The sound was enough to shock her out of the moment, and she drew back, eyes wide, a hand pressed to her swollen lips.

Callum looked like he was in a dream, eyes blinking. It took him another few seconds to return to the hackney and the busy street, and then she saw the flush of color rise in his cheeks. "I feel like I should apologize," he said, his voice husky, "but I don't want to. Should I say I am sorry, Miss Armstrong?"

She searched for the appropriate words but none came to her. For a moment she teetered on a precipice, knowing she should pull back and yet struggling to do so.

"No," she said at last. "I don't want you to say sorry, Mac-Kenzie."

He smiled then and reached out to tuck a strand of fair hair behind her ear. "Then I won't," he said.

CHAPTER TWELVE

C ALLUM LAY IN his bed and stared at the ceiling. Tonight was the practice ball, and the last of his fashionable clothing had arrived yesterday. His aunt had been aflutter with excitement and insisted that he make use of his uncle's valet—"He's kicking his heels at the moment, with no one to fuss over. You would be doing me a favor, Callum."

That had made him wonder if he would need to employ his own valet at Bonnyrigg. The thought of a stranger judging him was lowering, but then he wondered if perhaps Angus would take on the task? He could deal with Angus. And if it meant he could look the part of a duke-in-waiting, then what was the harm?

"I want to inspect you before you leave," Aunt Jennie had reminded him.

"You've seen me before."

"But not dressed up like a gentleman, Callum. That is something I have *never* seen before."

Now he had all day to think about tonight, and seeing Penelope again.

There had been no lessons since his visit to Mr. Doddington. He worried it was because of the kiss, and that their time apart would give her too much opportunity to mull over it. She might decide it was wrong. Callum's opinion differed. He believed it was the rightest thing he had ever done.

He had never felt like this about any other woman. Surely that meant something? He supposed his family would consider he

72

was infatuated, but Callum wasn't someone who was prone to such shallow emotions. He was sensible and level-headed, and the feelings he had developed for Penelope did not seem to be going away. Even if he eventually found this mythical wife and returned with her to Bonnyrigg, he was certain Penelope's memory would go home with him.

And he would mourn the loss of her every day.

He admitted to himself that right now the idea of marrying anyone who wasn't Penelope, of choosing some other woman to stand with him before the preacher and plight his troth . . . It just felt wrong in so many ways.

Apart from his personal feelings, Penelope was someone who would be able to deal with his aristocratic neighbors, host the dinners and soirees his father dreamed of, and shine bright in their moody Scottish winters. He could imagine her putting Sir Hector in his place, not by insulting him but by charming him into submission. There were so many reasons his family would applaud his choice of wife.

But there was also the problem of her past and her tarnished reputation. His parents would not approve of that any more than his aunt did. Word would soon circulate that his chosen wife had been the mistress of another man. Callum did not know the exact circumstances that had led Penelope down that road, but he was sure it had something to do with the tragic deaths of her parents and her guardianship of her young brother.

And if that was the case, he knew she had had no choice. She had been trapped in a bad situation, one that she had been doing her best to escape and then to make a new life for herself. But society was not so sympathetic, and he suspected his parents would be more inclined to listen to the negatives than the positives.

He sighed and ran a hand through his hair. There wasn't as much of it as yesterday. A barber had arrived to tame his dark locks, ready for his debut at the practice ball tonight. He was not looking forward to capering about, as Angus called it. He *was* looking forward to seeing Penelope and dancing with her.

Could he kiss her again? He longed to. His heart pounded and his blood heated at the thought of her mouth on his. Had she been remembering that moment too, aching for a repeat? She had seemed more than willing in the hackney, but Callum knew he had to tread carefully if he wanted to win her.

Because if marrying her was but a dream, then what was left? A brief affair? If he could not have her forever then why not a night? An hour?

If she was willing, then even one passionate encounter was better than nothing.

CALLUM WAS BIDING his time in the drawing room, waiting for his aunt's inspection of his outfit before he left for the ball. She had barely managed a glance at him before she was called away to solve a domestic crisis.

"A mouse!" she had exclaimed. "Evidently it is terrorizing the servants and only I can deal with it." She pointed at Callum. "Stay here. I won't be long."

The minutes ticked by. Callum tugged at his cravat, wishing it weren't so stiff and tight, but knowing he could not undo his uncle's valet's work. Would the guests at the ball give him *that* look? The "there he is, the Highland barbarian" look. Penelope would tell him to ignore them as being beneath him, and under no circumstances to feel the need to explain or retaliate. Which was all very well, but Callum was not used to being judged by strangers, and he did not like it.

Yes, he had been a fool at that fateful dinner at the Yeos'. Too much whisky and seeing that damned boar eyeing him from the table. One day he may laugh at it and think it amusing, but right now, he did not.

There was a sudden movement to one side of the room. A

flicker of grey running to shelter behind a rosewood chair.

A mouse! Probably *the* mouse.

Stealthily, he moved toward it, and leaning down, peered into the small gap between the back of the chair and the wall.

This close, it looked undersized and pinkish rather than grey, as if it had only recently left the nest. Under his gaze, it seemed to shrink even more, attempting to make itself invisible. Aunt Jennie's cat, Bothwell, was a tabby-and-white monster that roamed the house at will, and Callum wouldn't blame any mouse for being terrified.

When he was younger, Callum had had a large collection of creatures, and among them were several mice, so he was not at all afraid of them. He reached down, closing his hand gently about the small body.

"Come here, you wee thing," he whispered. "I won't let Jennie's cat harm you."

The mouse shivered but did not try to escape. He liked to think it understood him and trusted him. He straightened, still whispering to it, and became aware of his aunt's footsteps approaching across the marble floor of the hall.

Quickly, Callum slipped the mouse into the pocket of his evening jacket just as she entered the room.

"I have sent someone to fetch Bothwell," she told him. "He needs to earn his keep, and he has been getting very fat lately. He will soon hunt out this mouse."

Callum murmured agreement, as if the creature weren't safe in his care at this very moment.

Jennie came to a stop before him, running her gaze from his buckled shoes and stockings and silk breeches, up to his emerald-green waistcoat and forest-green jacket. His cravat was neatly tied, and his sapphire pin was placed squarely in the center of it, while his neatly trimmed hair was combed back from his forehead so that his closely shaven face was on full display.

"Do I pass?" he asked finally, not sure if he was amused or alarmed when she seemed unable to find her words.

To his horror, he saw that Jennie had tears in her eyes. She sniffed. "You look so much like your father, Callum. So braw. I wish he could see you."

He grinned and gave her an impulsive hug, which she returned warmly.

"All the same," she said, with a wrinkle between her brows, "I forgot to ask where this ball was being held. It is for practice, is it not?"

"That was what I was told. I am sure it is just what I need to get me ready."

"Hmm. If it is the sort of ball Miss Armstrong is invited to, then I'm not sure it is entirely proper."

He blinked, waiting for clarification.

Jennie made an impatient sound. "Really, Callum, do I need to explain? The woman's reputation is damaged, so if she is invited to this ball then the other guests must be of a similar standing. I understand why she wants you there. She seems sincere in her desire to give you the polish you need. You must feel familiar in such a setting, and she can put you through your paces on the floor, but all the same, I am not happy about it."

"I overheard her maid Selina calling it a Bohemian Ball," he admitted.

Jennie clicked her tongue. "Perhaps you shouldn't—" she began, and he could see her wavering.

Callum hurried to reassure her. "I promise I will be on my best behavior, Aunt Jennie. And you need no' worry. Did you forget I am a grown man, after all?"

"*That* is what worries me," she said. "You are a man and a handsome one, but in London ways, you are still an innocent, Callum. Imagine how furious Luna would be with me if anything untoward were to happen to you."

Untoward, he repeated silently to himself and tried not to chuckle. His aunt seemed to think that at twenty-five he knew nothing about the goings on at this so-called Bohemian Ball. While it was true that he wasn't a rake, like his brother Rory, neither was he an innocent virgin.

"Aunt Jennie, there is no reason for you to worry yourself," he said firmly. "Miss Armstrong wants me ready for your ball, to smooth over any rough edges I have left, so that I will not disgrace you. Or myself."

She sighed and then smiled. "Very well. Off you go then. Are you meeting Miss Armstrong there?"

"Yes."

"Perhaps you should take Angus with you?" she said, clearly having second thoughts again.

As far as Callum knew, Angus had other plans, but that wasn't the answer Jennie wanted to hear. "And have Angus glowering at me all night? Honestly, I will be fine. Nothing will happen, Aunt Jennie."

Jennie nodded like she wanted to believe it. "Very well. The coach is waiting for you outside. It has the Strathmore crest on the door, so if there is any question about your origins, people will be able to see you come from quality. You should not be made to feel lesser than them."

"I have never felt lesser than anybody until I came to London," he said wistfully.

She gave him another hug, and finally he was free to leave the house.

Once he was aboard the coach, Callum leaned back against the soft leather seat, feeling relieved. A ball wasn't something he was going to enjoy—he had never attended one before—but he knew all of the reasons he was attending. And more importantly, Penelope would be there with him. He smiled as he imagined her beautiful face as he danced with her. Tonight he hoped to have many dances with her in his arms, and perhaps he might even stumble a little or take a wrong step, just to ensure she paid more attention to him.

He was certainly a sad case where she was concerned.

As the coach rumbled over London's streets, Callum wished Angus were with him to share his pithy comments. But he had seen his manservant slipping out of the house in his best coat, with his hair washed and combed, which meant he was meeting a woman. Angus would not bother to smarten himself up for anyone else.

Callum smiled at the thought of the teasing he would give his friend when he returned.

CHAPTER THIRTEEN

NGUS STRODE WITH his usual confident swagger along
Jasmyne Street. His boots rang out. He wasn't wearing his
kilt because he didn't want to be noticed—he was still amazed
that such an ordinary piece of clothing had caused such a stir at
the park. He might look self-assured as he neared Miss Armstrong's front door, but he wasn't. This was the first time in a
long while he had set out to win over a woman, and never in his
wildest dreams had he imagined he would set his sights on an
English woman.

He hesitated as he lifted his hand to the knocker, and then
told himself not to be a coward, and let it fall. She might have
changed her mind anyway, he told himself. All of his primping
was probably for naught. Mabbe he should find a quiet drinking
house and drown his sorrows.

The door opened and Selina smiled up at him.

Angus was struck speechless. He wondered what it was about
her that turned him glaikit. She wasn't a beauty like her mistress,
and she wasn't curvy like the lassies he usually favored. She was
tall and skinny, and there was a sparkle in her blue eyes that
suggested he wouldn't always get his own way with her. Not
without some persuasion. But weren't the best things in life
worth working for?

Tonight she was wearing a cloak, the hood thrown back so
that her fair hair reflected in the glow of the streetlamp. And she
was smiling.

They had made this arrangement as soon as they'd learned about the Bohemian Ball. Callum and Penelope would both be elsewhere, so why shouldn't Angus and Selina meet up? It was innocent enough, which didn't explain Angus's jitters.

"Good evening," Selina said, when the silence drew on.

"Good evening to you, Miss Halliday," Angus replied, and took her hand and tucked it into his bent elbow. Inside her glove, her fingers were cold, and he kept hold of her with his larger hand, warming her.

They set off for their stroll.

Selina was tall enough for him not to crick his neck when he met her gaze, unlike Miss Armstrong, who was so wee a decent sized man would have to pick her up to kiss her.

He rather thought Callum wanted to do just that.

Guiltily, Angus admitted to himself that he should be keeping an eye on his young master, as the duke had ordered him to, but Callum was a grown man. And Angus was certain if he had suggested going along to the ball with him, Callum would have told him no. He could only hope Callum would not do anything that might further damage his good name in the eyes of the London *ton*. The boy—well, he was a man now—was a gentle soul with a kind heart and a strong sense of right and wrong. If he had a fault, it was being too impulsive. He jumped in when it would be better for him to wait and consider other options.

As for finding Callum the sort of wife his father wanted for him . . . Angus could only see unhappiness in that plan. The thought of having one of those sneering ladies living in Bonnyrigg, looking down on the MacKenzies, made him shudder.

"You are very quiet," Selina said at his side, as they strolled.

"I am thinking about my young master," Angus admitted. "I hope he doesna get up to any foolishness tonight."

"Ah." She snuggled close to his side and rested her chin on his arm so that she could look into his face. "I have a feeling he is partial to my mistress."

He raised his brows as if in surprise, although he had thought the same.

"And that is a good thing," Selina went on quickly. "She is beautiful and clever, and her life has not been a happy one. You saw what her brother is like?"

"I did," Angus growled.

Selina paused, choosing her words carefully. "She has perfect manners and knows which knife and fork and spoon to use at dinner. She can make conversation from the lowest of the low to the highest in the land. I have known her since she was a child, and as a young woman she could hold a room full of people in the palm of her hand. Her parents had friends who were peers of the realm, and they all found her charming. I assure you she would have no trouble in a duke's castle."

He gave her a faint smile. "I think I know where you are going with this."

"She would make Callum MacKenzie the perfect wife."

Angus shook his head regretfully. "She is no' what the duke has in mind."

They had reached a square with a garden. An owl called out as Selina sat down on a bench and Angus sat beside her. He breathed in the summer evening while he waited for her to answer.

"I understand that," she said. "But don't you think it is for your young master to choose his own wife? I have seen the way he looks at her."

"Mabbe, but she was a kept woman and her reputation will follow her over the border. It could turn out verra badly."

But even as he spoke, Angus wondered if that was true. Luna had fallen in love with Maxwell and married him when he was only a gamekeeper, so surely Callum's parents would understand what it meant to fall in love? Particularly if Callum chose a woman who was perfect in so many other ways. Could the duke and duchess overlook Penelope's reputation? Angus suspected Maxwell would be the stubborn one there—he was set on the perfect lady for his son.

Selina went on a little desperately. "If they met her, spoke to her, they would see—"

"Aye, I understand what you say, Selina, but it is out of my hands."

"Mine too," she said drearily.

Angus added in a grumpy voice, "I just hope Callum will no' get himself into mischief at the ball tonight. The lad seems to have the knack of getting into trouble wherever he goes."

Selina patted his arm. "I'm sure he will be perfectly fine," she soothed. "Miss Armstrong will keep him in line."

There was a pause, and Angus heard himself blurt out, "I'm glad you are here with me tonight. I am lonely in this big place."

He could have curled into a ball with embarrassment, but Selina laughed softly and leaned into him. "Then let us make the most of our night of freedom."

Angus searched her face in the moonlight. She looked as if she would welcome a kiss, so he kissed her.

"Why are *you* unwed?" he asked her, when he had regained his breath. "I canna believe you are not taken. A woman as kind and handsome as you."

Selina gave him a sad smile. "I was engaged once. I was to be married. You have heard how Penelope's parents died in a coach accident?"

He nodded. He had heard about that tragic event from Callum.

"My fiancé was also on the coach. He was Mr. Armstrong's valet and he was aboard when the accident happened. He died, too. I think..." she swallowed. "I think Penelope forgets sometimes that I was affected, too. We both lost people we loved on that day."

Angus didn't know what to say. He wrapped his arm around Selina and pulled her in tight against him. "My poor lassie," he murmured.

She took a moment to recover herself. "I do think of him sometimes—perhaps not as often as I once did—and imagine what my life might have been. We may have had children by now. I always wanted children."

"You can still have them," Angus said kindly.

But Selina shook her head. "I fear I am too old now. That door has closed, Angus."

Angus was ignorant about such matters as a woman's fertility but he hoped that was not so. Selina deserved happiness—she deserved to have her wishes fulfilled. As he bent his head to kiss her again, he wondered if he was the man to do it.

❧❧❧

CHAPTER FOURTEEN

T HE HOUSE LOOKED respectable enough from the outside, but once he passed the bruiser guarding the doorway, Callum could tell by the state of dress of some of the ladies that it was not respectable at all. He was glad his aunt was not by his side to see this—she would have dragged him home again. He was rather doubtful himself whether he should be here. His father, and certainly his mother, would not approve.

Callum averted his gaze from a woman whose breasts were all but bare. Was that a new fashion? He didn't think it would catch on in Bonnyrigg.

"Apologies," a breathless voice said at his side. "You are early, MacKenzie."

He looked down at Penelope, relieved that she was here. She was wearing a gown the color of his mother's favorite rose, a dusky pink, and although the neckline was lower than he had seen her wear before, it was certainly not as low as some of those here tonight. There was a sparkly necklace around her throat, and her hair was dressed with more sparkly stones, peeping out like stars from among her fair locks. A circlet of silk roses completed the look.

He wanted to tell her how beautiful she looked, but he found he had lost his words at the sight of her.

Penelope was casting glances about them at the assembly and now she pulled a face. "I *am* sorry to have brought you here, but it was the best I could do. This is definitely not Almack's, but at

84

least you will be able to practice dancing and conversing."

He blurted the words out. "Don't apologize. I will happily dance and converse with you, Miss Armstrong."

She met his eyes and smiled wryly. "Well, we shall see. You can dance with others, but I will be keeping a close watch. If anyone is presumptive enough to try to take you upstairs, I will rescue you."

There was that quiver inside him that happened whenever Penelope turned forceful. He wanted to tell her how much he would like her to rescue him but decided against it. Perhaps, if he was very good and didn't make any mistakes, he could win another kiss from her at the end of the evening.

There was a small orchestra, rather out of tune, but the couples who had taken to the floor were enjoying themselves. Penelope reached for his hand and led him into their midst. Callum slid his arm about her waist, and drew her in close, and they began to dance.

She seemed to be concentrating on watching his steps as he strove to do his best.

"You are very quiet," she said at last. "Have you no conversation, MacKenzie?"

"I am struck dumb by your beauty," he replied.

Penelope shot him a displeased look, but her cheeks were pink. "Rather overdoing it, MacKenzie?"

"It is only the truth," he said boldly.

Penelope let her gaze run over him as they parted, just their fingertips touching, and then resumed the dance. "You are rather beautiful yourself," she said in her droll way. "Has your aunt employed a valet?"

"My uncle's valet," he admitted. "He insisted I not leave the house until he was satisfied. I was too afraid to tell him nay."

Penelope smiled. "I am glad to hear it. A good valet should strike fear into the heart of his master." Her gaze seemed caught by something on the other side of the room and the pink flush in her cheeks grew more heated. Callum followed it to an alcove hidden behind a large potted plant. For a moment, he could hardly believe his eyes. He did not consider himself an innocent, but what he was seeing shocked him.

Of course he had been aware that, as well as dancing, there were other activities taking place in the room. Couples kissing and fondling and vanishing up the staircase. But now he could see that in the alcove, there was a woman on her back on a settee with her skirts thrown up, and between her legs was a gentleman, his buttocks bare and pumping.

His face must have shown his feelings at such a vulgar sight because Penelope squeezed his hand, and said once more, her voice full of shame. "I *am* sorry. This is one of the more scandalous balls. If I had had a choice I would never—"

"No, I . . ." He cleared his throat. "I am just a wee bit surprised."

"We can leave, but first we should make the most of the music and the dance floor," she said in a practical voice, and they returned to their dance.

Callum thought this all rather strange. Penelope seemed more worried about his feelings than caring about the open debauchery around her. He could not imagine his mother being so unruffled—she would have taken a broomstick to the couple in the alcove—and as for his sister Cat, she would have been horrified. But as shocked as he was, Callum found that as they continued to dance together, the brush of her skirts against his legs, and the little wrinkle of concentration between her brows, her presence in his arms, held his attention significantly more than the goings on around them.

After a pause, she said, "You are very good at dancing, MacKenzie, but you need to learn to converse while doing so. Just some idle chit-chat, if that is all you can manage. Your partner will not care about deeper matters. The weather is a good fallback."

"Do you always tell your clients to talk about the weather?"

She laughed. "Yes. Everyone in London has an opinion on the

weather. I am sure it is the same in Scotland."

"I hope my wife is not averse to a variety of different weathers. Bonnyrigg can be calm and sunny in the morning, only to turn wet and windy by noon. And then come evening, there may be a blizzard."

She smiled but she was watching him closely. "You love it," she declared.

"Bonnyrigg? I do. I would not want to live anywhere else."

"Then you must find someone who will learn to love Bonnyrigg for your sake, if not her own."

He thought about that. "I would not ask anyone to playact. That way lies misery for both parties, surely?"

She considered her answer. "I think if you love someone enough you can see a place through their eyes. Is that not just as good as loving it yourself?"

The dance had ended and another one began. Callum noticed a rakish looking gentleman hovering nearby, wanting to take his place with Penelope, and he gave him one of his formidable glares. The man turned around and hurried off.

Satisfied, he turned back to find Penelope watching him, her grey eyes sparkling. "Very good," she said, her voice breathless and trying not to laugh. "That worked a treat. Lord Freith will not bother us again."

"Did you know him?" Callum asked with a frown. "Did you want to dance with Lord Freith?"

Penelope shook her head. "I do not." She paused and then added, "He was one of the gentlemen who made me an offer after Lord Muir died."

The thought of her with Freith caused a hot wave of fury to rise in Callum. It consisted of jealousy and rage, and a possessiveness that almost frightened him. She wasn't his, he reminded himself—as much as he wanted her to be his. And besides, he suspected she was quite able to take care of herself.

Callum was distracted however, and he spun her about a little too vigorously as they took the corner. Before he could apologize, he felt something wriggling in his jacket pocket.

The mouse!

He had completely forgotten it. The little creature had stayed quietly in hiding all this time, but now it seemed that it had reached the limit of its endurance.

Before he could reach in to soothe it, the mouse leapt from its confinement and ran down the leg of his breeches, then sprang to the floor and scampered across it.

Never in his life could Callum have imagined that something so small and harmless could cause such pandemonium. Women began screaming and jumping about, while the men who weren't doing the same were either looking around in bewilderment or clumsily attempting to capture the mouse. It was far too swift for any of them. Before Callum could begin to move to block its escape, his little friend had reached the doorway and vanished.

Amidst the shrieks and shouts, and the jarring notes as the orchestra came to an abrupt halt, Callum turned and met Penelope's eyes.

She looked amazed. "Did that mouse just come out of your pocket?"

Callum thought about fibbing, but there seemed no point if she had seen it. "Yes. I put it in there at Aunt Jennie's to save it from Bothwell, and then I forgot about it."

"Bothwell?" she asked faintly.

"Her cat." He leaned in closer, suddenly concerned, "You are not afraid of them, are you? They are harmless enough. Unless they make their home in your pantry, of course."

The noise around them had settled down, and a woman Callum assumed to be the hostess was reassuring people. Callum wondered if he should confess, but even as he considered it, Penelope took a firm grip on his arm.

"Best not to," she warned him quietly. "You are in enough trouble as it is, MacKenzie."

The orchestra began to play again, more out of tune than ever, but neither Callum nor Penelope moved to resume their dance.

"I'm sorry. It was instinctive. I have so many pets at Bonnyrigg, creatures I have rescued and tried to nurse back to health. Some of them can't care for themselves, so I keep them safe."

She watched him, fascinated. "What sort of pets?"

"A blind squirrel," he said easily, knowing them all by heart. "A wee fallow deer whose mother died. Five lambs and a crow with one leg."

Penelope stared at him a moment more as if she was having trouble believing him, and then suddenly she began to laugh. At first she tried to stifle the sound with her hand, but when she couldn't, she made haste to leave the room, and worried and confused, Callum followed her out into the hallway.

A lady in a bright-red wig gave them a sympathetic look. "I don't blame you for being frightened, my dear. A mouse! 'Tis a fearsome thing."

Penelope didn't pause. She climbed the staircase, only pausing halfway to gasp for air as she continued to shake with laughter. Callum climbed, too, staying close in case she needed him, until they reached the landing. There was a hallway and one of the doors was open, and she went inside. Callum saw that it was a bedchamber, which did not seem appropriate, but he thought that at least they could be private now.

He closed the door and sank down into a chair while he waited for Penelope to recover herself.

It seemed to be taking a while, but he was happy to wait. He thought that perhaps her laughter wasn't just about him and his mouse, but a culmination of many things that had been weighing upon her. Her emotions had reached a tipping point and she was letting them out. Which was a *good* thing in his opinion—better to laugh than to cry.

Penelope had thrown herself onto the four poster bed and buried her face in the pillow, but he could see her shoulders shaking. After a time, he said, "I get the sense that gentlemen in London do not keep pets."

She lifted her head and wiped her eyes. Her face was flushed and alive with humor. "They do," she said shakily, "but perhaps not quite so many. A dog or a cat. Certainly not a—a crow with one leg." Then she took a deep, steadying breath and sat up. "Callum, you truly do amaze me."

He brightened. "Do I?"

She looked at him again, opened her mouth and then closed it and shook her head. "It wasn't a compliment," she said gently.

"Oh." He tried not to be downcast. "It is because I lived my early years in the forests of Scotland," he said. "My father always had some injured animal or other to care for, and I followed in his footsteps. If my wife does not like it . . . Well, I could not marry someone who did not."

"You are kind," she said firmly. "I would not want to take that from you. There is already so much unkindness in the world."

"I cannot allow something to suffer when I can alleviate their pain."

She nodded. Her hair had fallen out of its arrangement, and the silk flowers were hanging drunkenly over one ear. And yet Callum thought she was the most beautiful woman he had ever seen.

He stood up and went to the side of the bed and looked down at her while she looked back at him. They both held their breaths, and then he stooped over her, took her face in his hands and kissed her.

It was only when she stiffened beneath him that he realized he was being forward. She would surely push him away, or berate him in that prim voice he secretly enjoyed, but to his surprise, she did neither.

Penelope put her hands over his larger ones and kissed him back.

CHAPTER FIFTEEN

PENELOPE KNEW THIS was against all her self-imposed rules. Her very crucial self-imposed rules. She wasn't sure how she had reached this point—although a sly voice in her head told her that she had known all along this was going to happen. She should pull away now and tell him no. She should get up and go home. He didn't need any more instruction on the dance floor; he was perfect as he was. The Bohemian Ball had deteriorated far quicker than she'd feared, and if not for the mouse, she would have drawn the lesson to a close. But there *was* the mouse and now here she was, alone in a bedchamber with a man she had found insanely attractive from the first instant she saw him.

Stopping felt as if it might very well kill her.

His mouth against hers was tender and yet masterful. No lessons needed there either. She allowed herself to be drawn into the heat and excitement of the kiss. There was a curl low in her belly that she hadn't felt for years, and she craved more.

Her body ached for this man.

Placing her palm flat against his chest, she began to explore the hard muscle and bone beneath the layers of his clothing. Suddenly, more than anything, she wanted his naked flesh against hers, the intimate press of their bodies, sliding together. The ache inside her grew until the longing to have it assuaged was too loud to ignore. It had been too long since she'd felt the pleasure of physical love, and to feel it with *this* man . . . she couldn't wait any longer.

He nuzzled against her ear, catching the lobe between his teeth gently, before dipping his face to her neck and sucking at her skin. Shivers ran up and down her back, and she gasped, arching so that he had better access. The neckline of her gown was not overly low, not like some of the women here who were showing all they had, but it was low enough for him to lick a line across the swell of her breasts.

Her nipples hardened into painful points, rubbing against the stiff cloth of her bodice, desperate for his mouth. His tongue. Half dazed, she looked up to meet his eyes. Heat and longing shone in their dark depths—a match for her own.

"Will you allow me?" he asked in a voice grown husky with desire. His hands rested on her shoulders and slid around to the hook at her back, teasing the fastening but not opening it yet. Waiting for her consent.

No, she thought. *This is an awful mistake.* But her voice refused to obey her.

"Yes," she said.

He smiled, and his fingers worked at the fastenings with swift movements. In an instant, her bodice sagged and her breasts were free. He drew in an appreciative breath.

She told herself she would only allow him to touch her once, just once, and then she would put a stop to this. She *must* put a stop to this. Even when Selina had told her to make the most of her time with him, she had thought her rules would keep her safe. They hadn't, and it was too late, and suddenly she didn't care. Whatever happened afterward, she would remember this night forever.

"So beautiful," he whispered, and then he was sucking and lathing with his tongue, and she lost any strength she had to push him away.

It felt wonderful, and once again, that heat unfurled inside her belly, the ache between her thighs, a physical response of her longing for him to join with her.

For three years she had been so responsible, so strict with

herself, but now she lost it all. Everything crumbled before him. She surrendered. With a soft groan, she held his head closer, arching into his mouth.

He had been kneeling on the bed, but now he leaned back and began to strip off his clothes with a complete disregard for his new finery. She didn't scold him; instead, she helped him, her hands trembling with urgency, until she found bare flesh. His chest made her mouth water and she leaned in and ran the tip of her tongue over his warm skin, and then took his nipple in her mouth.

He gasped and reached to gently cup the back of her head, wanting to keep her there. But she wanted more of him. She licked up to his throat, tongue tracing the dip there before seeking his strong jaw. Tasting him. He swallowed, took a breath, and reached to fumble with his breeches. When she looked down, she could see the hard line of his cock, pushing against the silk.

She had meant to help him, but he distracted her with kisses, desperate and passionate, and for a time she forgot anything but the heat and taste of his mouth on hers. It might have been enough, but Penelope was no innocent. She was aware of what pleasures could be had with a man, and she craved them with *this* man.

"I want you inside me," she said.

"God, yes," he muttered.

She pushed him back onto the bed and he raised his head to watch as she unfastened his breeches and reached in to close her hand around the hot length of him. He looked feverish, she thought, as she lowered her head and took the tip into her mouth, sucking. He groaned so loudly she thought they might hear him downstairs.

His chest was rising and falling, and he arched his hips, and she knew if she kept on, he would spill. And what a pity that would be when her body was crying out for his. Penelope knelt over him, straddling his hips and lifting her skirts out of the way.

Callum growled out something that sounded like, "So bonny." He slid his hands over her knees and up her thighs. Up and up, until his thumbs brushed her most intimate flesh. She gasped. He gripped her bottom and had lifted her up as if she weighed nothing, and then his mouth closed on the throbbing nerves between her legs.

Quite simply, it was ecstasy. This was something that had never been done to her before, although she had heard of it from others. When his tongue lathed around her bud and sucked the responsive flesh into his mouth, she could not be quiet. She cried out as pleasure soared through her, again and again, leaving her lightheaded.

Penelope went tumbling amongst the stars, the universe topsy-turvy about her, spinning endlessly. Or so it seemed. When she came back to herself again, catching her breath, blinking, she found she was sprawled on the bed and he was now above her.

"So beautiful," he whispered, his eyes shining. "I want you so much."

There was something she should say, something she had meant to do, but her mind was empty of words, so instead she reached up to kiss him. At the same time, she stretched down to stroke his cock, which at some point he had completely freed from the constraint of his breeches, and he groaned.

"Are you sure?" he asked breathlessly.

She was already positioning him at the entrance to her welcoming sheath.

"Take me," she said.

He filled her, sliding easily inside, and the passion she had thought spent began to build again. He moved and so did she, gripping him with hands and legs and body, feeling like she would never get close enough to this man. Whatever might happen tomorrow did not matter. Right now, there was no tomorrow, only this intimate, magical moment between the two of them.

He was a powerful man who could easily have taken her without care for her own pleasure, but he didn't. He was no brute. He was patient, taking his time. A bead of sweat ran down the side of his face. "Feels so good," he groaned. "Perfect. I knew it would be. I don't want it to stop."

He was too sweet and suddenly she could not bear it. She did not want him to love her—that would be disastrous for them both.

"I do not give lessons in fucking," she said crudely. "Only manners and etiquette."

Instead of being hurt or insulted, he grinned. "I do not need lessons in fucking," he growled, and thrust deeper, brushing against some spot inside that made her cry out with aching pleasure.

God, he was good. She wanted to laugh with joy, but just then her orgasm caught her and she was gasping and arching against him as he reached his own crescendo. For a time they lay, panting and wrung out. Her muscles seemed to have ceased to exist, and he was heavy on top of her. But she didn't mind. She was sorry when he rolled to her side.

She could feel his gaze admiring her, on her face and her bare breasts. She turned to face him.

"I suspect you were no virgin," she said drolly.

"You suspect right." He looked up at her almost coyly through his dark lashes. "I have had my share of girls, me and Rory both. He has had more, and Donal loves only one girl and he is true to her. But Penelope, I have never had anyone like you. You are . . ."

His voice trailed off as if he had thought better of his next words.

What had he been about to say? You are the love of my life? Stay with me forever? She knew he must not love her, and their time together was finite. Why did she long to hear those words from him? What was wrong with her that she would destroy her future and his for the sake of a vow no man had ever made to her?

His face turned serious, because he had guessed at some of what she was thinking.

"Don't send me away, not yet," he said. "We have more lessons. More time."

It was on the tip of her tongue to tell him there could be no more lessons, but instead she lifted her hand to touch his cheek, cupping the warm flesh and feeling his whiskers rasp against her palm.

"It cannot be more than a brief affair," she said seriously. "Do you understand? Even so, I am risking—"

"Nothing," he assured her. "I will not tell, and we will be careful. No one will know, Penelope."

Wouldn't they? There were so many ways in which this could go wrong, but she already knew she was going to do it. It was worth taking the gamble to be with him again, and as many times as they could manage, before it was over.

"I am a fool for agreeing," she said, even as she stretched up to kiss him.

His mouth was warm with promises, and Penelope wanted to believe every one of them.

CHAPTER SIXTEEN

CALLUM ARRIVED AT Jasmyne Street the next morning, his body still humming but his head clear. He should have been tired after last night—he had not reached home until early morning—but instead he was more alive than he had been since he'd arrived in London. He wanted to see Penelope again. He *needed* to see her in a way that left him breathless.

Their time together had felt like something exceptional. Did she feel the same? Last night she had agreed to an affair, but this morning she might have changed her mind. He hoped not. If an affair was all she had to offer him then he would take it, but he admitted to himself that he wanted more. Deep in his secret heart, he wanted a great deal more.

"MacKenzie."

Penelope's voice sounded behind him in the sitting room, and he spun around, a smile he couldn't hold in on his face.

She was not smiling. She was watching him with that careful caution he knew meant she did not want him to see what she was thinking. That, and the shadows under her eyes and the way in which her hair was drawn back in a severe style he had not seen before, did not bode well for any sort of future between them.

She was frowning as her gaze wandered over him. He looked down at himself and realized then that in his rush to get here, to see her again, he had dressed in a rush. Compared to last night's splendor, he must look like a ragbag.

"MacKenzie, you are disheveled," she said in her forceful

voice. "Your shirt is creased and your jacket ill-made. Is it one of your old ones? At least your boots are clean."

"Angus makes sure of that," he admitted.

"Perhaps Angus should supervise the rest of you," she said. Her judgmental gaze dropped to his pantaloons. "These are very baggy," she said critically. "The fashion is for them to be as tight as is bearable to the wearer. What about the inexpressibles Mr. Doddington made for you?"

"They escaped my mind."

"I can see that."

"These were to hand, and I was in a hurry," he admitted, wondering if they were really going to discuss his choice of pantaloons. He sought for some criticism of *her* appearance, but she was perfect as usual, and he could only find one.

"I don't like your hair," he said abruptly. "You look like a headmistress about to give me the cane."

She raised an eyebrow, but instead of engaging with that thought, she said, "Sit down."

He sat and she arranged herself opposite him. By now he was beginning to wonder if last night had been a dream because this woman was so removed from the abandoned creature he had held in his arms. And she was not making it easy for him to find a way to bring up the subject. It was as if she had locked their intimate evening away and was refusing to acknowledge it.

"I think you will need to spend more time and thought on your appearance, MacKenzie," she was saying. "What woman would shackle herself to you as you are now? Presentation is very important when it comes to attracting a wife."

"Thank you," he said, trying not to grit his teeth. "I am not used to worrying about my appearance overmuch. We do not have many social occasions to dress up for at Bonnyrigg."

"Well, if you marry the sort of woman you have described to me, you will have many more social occasions. You need to prepare yourself."

He groaned in real despair, and she narrowed her eyes at him.

"Don't you want to be admired and looked up to by your neighbors? I thought that was the point."

"My father wants us to rise in the world, but I'm not sure he wants to be admired. He does not need the admiration of others to be the man he is, and neither do I."

She blinked at him. "Callum," she began, with a sigh, "how can I change you for the better if you will not listen?"

"I am listening," he retorted.

"At least have some pantaloons fitted to your figure and—and shape," she said, unexpectedly stammering on the words. "It would be such an improvement. That garment is so very loose."

"It's getting tighter by the minute," he muttered.

Her eyes narrowed. "What is that supposed to mean?"

"It's that voice you use when you are scolding me. It . . . I find it very stimulating."

She went still. "Callum," she said.

"Penelope," he replied.

And then with a sound very like a whimper, she stood and launched herself into his arms. Surprised and elated, Callum caught her, gripping her waist as she leaned over him, her mouth already seeking his.

And just like that, he was lost. The sensation of her lips against his, the desperate need that was right there, was more important than anything else. The mask she had been wearing was stripped away and the woman from last night was back, a little more frantic perhaps, but she was in his arms just as he had hoped she would be when he set off in a rush this morning.

She was already fumbling at his pantaloons, the ones she had just been berating him for, and he was hard and ready.

"I can't believe I'm doing this," she said in wonder. "I must be insane."

"Welcome to the asylum." He kissed her so that he could silence whatever else was coming from her mouth. It was too late to stop, it really was.

He lifted her, his hands finding the soft shape of her thighs and buttocks, adjusting her so that she was in the right position. She groaned softly as his cock brushed against that place he had discovered last night was her most sensitive and slid inside. She clung to him, murmuring encouragement, urging him to go faster. Already he could feel himself close.

"Hurry," she panted. "Selina is bringing tea."

Callum gave a painful laugh, and in the next instant they had reached their crescendo. She trembled, her eyelids fluttering as he tried not to shout out aloud to the world just how wonderful this was.

She was quicker to recover than him. She was already climbing off him, smoothing her skirts, pushing at her hair, which he was glad to see was no longer looking so severe. With trembling hands, he buttoned himself up and then stood, a little shakily, trying to get a grip on his emotions.

"Penelope," he began, not knowing how to contain the words clamoring to be said. He thought he might be going to tell her how much he admired her—because God knew he could not say the *L* word. Nor could he say that he wanted to marry her and take her back to Bonnyrigg and have his way with her several times a day.

His strong urge to say all of those things filled him with horror. Penelope would cancel their lessons immediately and send him on his way. Perhaps it was just as well Selina knocked on the door at that moment and entered.

She froze in the doorway, the tray full of teapot and cups rattling violently in her hands. Her gaze went from Penelope to Callum and back again, but she said nothing. After a pause, she continued into the room, chattering about the cake she had made and how she hoped Callum would like it. After setting the tray on the table, she straightened, looking rather flushed, and she hurried to the door. It closed quietly behind her.

Penelope put her hands over her face. "You see what you have done," she said in a muffled voice. "Now I will never hear the end of it from her. After all my promises never to allow one of my clients to step beyond the boundaries I have set."

Callum thought he should be insulted. Was he really just one of her clients? He had been believing himself to be more. Deciding to take a lighter approach, he reached for a cup and poured in the tea and added milk.

She had dropped her hands and was watching him, and now she glared. "You should add the milk first," she said. "You must always add the milk first."

Confused, he froze with the cup halfway to his lips. "I never add the milk first!"

"It is the rule," she continued, eyes sparkling with righteous indignation.

"There are no rules!" he said stubbornly. "I like to add the milk last, and I willna change."

"MacKenzie, what use is it to tell you things if you refuse to do them?"

Now they were shouting over each other, and suddenly Callum had had enough.

He leaned over the table and kissed her.

She seemed to be about to push him away, and then instead she caught hold of the lapels of his jacket and held him there. Their kiss grew more heated, and when she tugged him closer, he knocked against the table and the tea tray, and there was a crash as everything fell to the floor.

He didn't care, and neither, it seemed, did she. Once again, they were too insatiable for each other to stop.

Even when he heard the door open and Selina's, "What on earth . . . ?" he couldn't bring himself to behave like the gentleman he was supposed to be. Anyway, Selina left again immediately and they were once more alone.

"We truly are insane," Penelope said with quiet amazement, pausing their frantic kisses to look up at him. He was on the settee now, lying on top of her.

"I am happy with that," he replied. "Insanity suits us."

"Callum . . ."

"No, I will hear no more from those lovely lips. I am going to take you now, and this time I am going to make it last."

"Oh God," she moaned. They were the last coherent words she spoke.

AFTER CALLUM HAD gone, Penelope could hardly bear to look at Selina. The other woman seemed about to burst with excitement. And laughter.

"I knew it!" she kept saying gleefully. "As soon as I saw him, I just knew it!"

Penelope wasn't sure what it was Selina knew, but she was certain that at some point she would have to hear all about it. Right now she preferred to be alone with her wildly racing thoughts. One moment she was castigating herself for her stupidity, and the next she was remembering Callum's kisses and his touch, and his handsome face flushed with desire as he looked down upon her.

His eyes . . . She could look into his eyes forever.

Madness or not, neither of them could stop themselves. But shouldn't Penelope be the one to stop? Wasn't she supposed to be in charge?

"You have a right to enjoy yourself," Selina reminded her quietly.

Penelope looked up and found the other woman seated opposite, watching her challengingly.

"You have given up a great deal over the years. For Mortimer, mainly." Selina swallowed, knowing plain speaking might not be what Penelope wanted to hear. "I think it is time you thought of what *you* wanted."

"What I want and what I don't want have nothing to do with it," Penelope replied, but without her usual fire. "I have a livelihood to maintain."

"MacKenzie is only here for a short time, and then he will be gone."

She had never felt so low in her life. "Yes."

"Then again, maybe—"

"There is no *maybe*," Penelope retorted. "Callum MacKenzie needs a wife suited to his position and his father's ambitions. I am not that person, as you well know, Selina!"

Something in her voice must have registered with her friend. Penelope had heard the ache in it, the desperate wish that things were different, but what was the point? They weren't different, they could never be different, and she must learn to accept it.

Selina shook her head. "You are too hard on yourself. Why don't you ask MacKenzie what he thinks? He might surprise you."

Penelope shook her head. She couldn't allow herself to hope. Her dreams would only be dashed. She knew better than to see her world through an idealistic lens. "My career as a teacher of etiquette is probably over anyway," she said dully. "Have there been any more enquiries?"

Selina admitted there had not.

"I am sure if you spoke to MacKenzie . . ." she began.

"No. I will not do that. At the moment, he might believe himself infatuated with me, because that is all it is, but it would soon wear off. And what then? I would have ruined him, taken away his dreams and those of his parents, and be sentenced to a life of misery in cold, miserable Bonnyrigg. Is that what you want for me, Selina?"

Selina shook her head. "Of course it isn't," she said, her eyes suspiciously bright. "But you could make it work, I know you could. You could charm the MacKenzies into welcoming you into their lives. They would love you, as you deserve to be loved."

Penelope had nothing to say to that—she could not get the words past the lump in her throat. The problem was, it *did* sound wonderful. A life where she was part of a family, with a husband who loved her and perhaps even children, if it wasn't too late. But then what of Mortimer? And what of her tarnished reputation? Someone would find out, and word would spread and she wasn't sure she could bear to see the disappointment in the eyes of those she may by then have grown to love.

Better not to risk it.

A fling, yes. An affair, that was a possibility. Then she could store up the memories of MacKenzie and their time together, so that she could dust them off in the years to come. Take each one out like a precious jewel. And remember.

CHAPTER SEVENTEEN

Angus had been looking forward to his next outing with Selina. This time they were meeting during daylight hours. Selina had been appalled to learn he had not seen any of the famous London sights. "At least let me show you the Tower of London," she said.

Angus was agreeable to most of her suggestions, as long as he could spend time with her. He had discovered he enjoyed her company a great deal. She was amusing and made him laugh, and for two people from such vastly different backgrounds, they seemed to be remarkably like-minded when it came to their thoughts and opinions. He acknowledged to himself that he would miss her when he returned with Callum to Bonnyrigg.

If the lad found a wife, that was.

It seemed that once again his and Selina's thoughts were following the same path, and it wasn't long before she mentioned her mistress. That was when he remembered that although their opinions may be mostly compatible, there was one subject on which they could not agree.

"I know Penelope is smitten with MacKenzie, although she refuses to admit it. I saw them. They were . . ." She shot him a sideways glance, her cheeks pink. "Well, I won't tell you. I'm sure you can guess."

Angus's eyes widened as he caught her meaning. "You dinna say! Where was this?"

"In the sitting room. They are quite shameless," but she was smiling.

"Callum has seemed verra cheerful, and now I know why." Angus thought a moment. "Mabbe it will run its course. These things often do."

She glanced at him as if she wanted to ask how he knew and interrogate him about his own encounters with women but didn't quite dare. He didn't mind if she did, he wasn't ashamed of his past, but those brief encounters seemed tawdry when compared with his feelings for Selina.

"What if it doesn't?" she said. "Run its course, I mean."

Angus considered. "I'm sorry, but I still dinna think the duke will be happy if his son comes home with such a wife."

Selina looked annoyed. "You say it like she worked in some horrid brothel! She is beautiful and intelligent and would make MacKenzie very happy."

"Aye, but there is the small matter of her being another man's mistress."

Selina took umbrage at that. "The term is 'old man's darling', and that was only because she had no choice. If he had decided to help her and her brother financially, without strings attached, then everything would have been all right. But no, he had to be selfish. So many men are."

Angus thought that was probably true and wondered if it was aimed at him. He decided to ignore it. "That still doesna change things, Selina."

She wanted to argue, he could see that, but she didn't. She just looked downhearted. "No," she said, and looked up at Angus, her blue eyes moist with unshed tears. "I just want her to be happy. More than anyone else I know, she deserves it."

His heart ached for her as he said gently, "I know ye do. I just don't know how it can be brought about."

Selina thought a moment. They had been wandering through the Tower and were now standing in the room where the crown jewels were kept. For all her talk of them earlier, she did not seem to notice. "Does Callum never stand up to his father? Could he choose Penelope and say to hell with the world?"

Angus chuckled. "The duke is not a tyrant. But he feels he must do all he can to raise the family up, because it was his marriage to the old duke's daughter that caused them to be looked down upon. He was a gamekeeper, and that is what people remember. He wants his son to have a wife who can win them over."

"But that is exactly what Penelope can do!" Selina cried.

Several people looked in their direction, and she shrank into Angus's side.

"Aye, I see that," he said quietly, smiling down at her, "but it is not up to us. Callum and your mistress must find their own way out of this maze."

He could tell she wasn't happy with that, but Angus refused to be further drawn into the tangle.

"Now show me your favorite jewel," he said.

To her credit, Selina shook off her anxiety and was soon chattering away again. He listened, smiling and looking awed at the right times. He felt for her, and for Callum and Penelope, but what was to be done? The duke would not be happy if his son brought home a woman who did not fit in with his future plans, although Angus had to wonder if Maxwell was not being rather hypocritical.

Over the years, Angus had learned that interfering in the lives of others, even if it was well meant, did not end well.

"Will you take some supper with me after this?" he said abruptly. "It is your day off, isn't it? You do not have to go back by dark?"

Selina smiled with delight. "Yes, I would love to take supper with you."

"I have been looking forward to your company and I don't want it to end," he said, the words a little stilted because his heart was pounding. "You say that Penelope deserves to be happy, but Selina, so do you."

She was gazing at him as if he was everything she could wish for, which embarrassed him even more. Angus was well aware of his faults, and he had never imagined he would find a woman he cared about like this. One thing he knew for sure: He would be willing to do almost anything to see Selina Halliday smile.

CHAPTER EIGHTEEN

PENELOPE TOOK A sip from her Worcester blue-and-white teacup—she had told Callum that the set had been her mother's and was one of the few things she had left of her. Unfortunately, almost all the cups and saucers had been broken in her move to Jasmyne Street. Callum had decided that if he had his way, he would buy her several tea sets, one for each day of the week.

They were in her sitting room, and Penelope had been instructing him on the length of time one should spend when calling upon a lady.

Callum had pretended to be listening.

"I thought for our next lesson we should ride out of the city. A picnic in the country is always a popular outing during the warmer months. Many a romance has had its beginnings at a picnic in the country."

Callum was more than happy to oblige. He wondered if she was aware what that picnic would lead to? What their every moment together lately seemed to lead to?

To Penelope's apparent surprise, their affair had not cooled down. "I thought we would be past this by now," she had gasped earlier when he had pressed her against the wall and lifted her until she could hook her legs around his hips. They had then spent several very pleasurable moments locked together.

Callum had not expected his ardor to cool. He was already heating up again. After they had both groaned out their pleasure, she had stroked her fingers through his hair, her eyes closed, like she had forgotten that she was meant to be teaching him the society rules she thought him sadly lacking.

Those words had been on the tip of his tongue again, the ones he already knew would put a stop to these passionate interludes. He wanted to declare his undying love for her and beg her to marry him, but how could he when he knew she would put an end to things?

Callum didn't want that. He couldn't bear it.

His teacup rattled as he set it down on the saucer, and she narrowed her eyes, clearly worried he would damage the precious thing.

Callum cleared his throat. "Will I be expected to take part in many picnics?"

"Some. Everyone enjoys the outdoors when it is fine. Don't worry, apart from dressing nicely and making polite conversation, there will be no great effort required on your part. There are servants to help serve the food and pack it away again."

"I will not have to hunt a plump pheasant for our luncheon then?"

She shot him a reproving look.

Callum wanted to keep her for as long as it was possible, so he was forever thinking up ways in which he needed her help. Even after Aunt Jennie's ball, he wanted to continue his lessons. Even after he found a perfect wife. But the trouble with that was he could not imagine any wife more perfect than Penelope Armstrong.

If only he could persuade her to believe in him. In herself.

THE COUNTRYSIDE WAS green and pleasant, but with nothing of the wild beauty of his home. He knew in his heart that it could not compare to the forests and mountains of Bonnyrigg, just as no woman could compare with Penelope. And yet he admitted that this scenery was pleasant in its own tame way.

"Very pretty," he said, when Penelope pointed out a view to him that she said was famous, although he couldn't help but sound patronizing. No wonder she gave him a look.

Behind them, Angus snorted a laugh at something Selina said. They had brought their servants with them for propriety's sake, but Angus and Selina seemed more interested in each other than in acting as chaperones to their master and mistress.

"When you are courting your wife, you will be with a group of people," Penelope said brightly, although he could not help but notice her face was pale with shadows under her eyes. "They will consist of her friends or members of her family. How you deport yourself will be very important, and when you ask for her hand, any mistakes you make will be remembered."

"Well, that's good to know," he murmured.

Another of those looks, which only made him want to grab her and kiss her until she forgot all about her lessons.

"Ah, there is the ruin I was talking about," she went on, pointing toward a few stones and a tower with vines growing up it. "The castle was 'slighted' by Cromwell."

"Oh aye, that is what they call blowing it into wee bits, do they?" Angus spoke up.

Selina shushed him.

"It would be nice if you were to learn some of the history of the places you visit," Penelope went on, ignoring the interruption. "You can impress your future wife in that way."

"Won't she know the history herself?" Callum said. "It would be arrogant of me to tell her what she already knows."

"She will probably pretend ignorance," Penelope replied. "Girls . . . women are taught not to be too forward in such circumstances."

"Pretend they are silly, do ye mean?" Angus interrupted again. "MacKenzie doesna want a silly wife, do you lad?"

Callum shot him a grateful look. "I do not!"

"I do not mean she is silly," Penelope said in a long-suffering voice. "She is clever enough not to want to be thought forward."

"I rather like a woman who is forward." Callum smiled. "I like a woman who tells me what to do. I may not always do it, but I like to be told."

There was a silence after that, and he was glad when they stopped the carriage and set about arranging the picnic. He could hear Angus's deep murmur and Selina's lighter voice, but Penelope was deep in her own thoughts again. He glanced sideways at her and found her glancing back at him.

"Do you mean that?" she asked him abruptly. "About liking me to tell you what to do? Most gentlemen would hate it."

"Well, I am not most gentlemen," he reminded her. "And I do like it. When your voice gets all determined and disdainful . . . I like it very much."

She couldn't mistake his meaning. Her eyes widened slightly before she returned to her work of unpacking the basket. But he thought there was a little smile on her lips.

After they had finished most of the cheese, cold meat, and bread, and washed down the strawberries and confections with a chilled Chablis, Callum lay back on the grass, replete. He gazed up at the soft, blue sky above him. The air felt pleasantly warm, and he had removed his jacket and his necktie—be damned to etiquette—and with a full belly, he was thinking about a snooze.

Unfortunately, Penelope had other ideas. She seemed determined to cram as many lessons as possible into the moment. He supposed she knew their time together was coming to an end, and he understood she wanted to make him as perfect a gentleman as it was possible for him to be, but he wished she would stop. Occasionally her voice had a manic edge to it, a panicky note that made him want to wrap her in his arms and tell her, *This doesn't have to end. Marry me.*

After several observations about him eating far too much, and a brief argument after his retort that him eating too much was a compliment to his hostess, she changed tack.

"What would you be doing if you were at Bonnyrigg? Tell me about it. Make me intrigued. Make me want to go there with you, Callum." She stopped, realizing her mistake. "Make the woman you choose to marry want to go there."

He pretended not to notice her slip of the tongue. "And how do I do that? I could tell her that it can be a grim place in the winter. Cold and damp, and the castle has drafts that feel like icy fingers. My mother tries to keep us warm with fires in all the rooms, and a roaring one in the great hall, but it is no easy task. I am used to it, but visitors often complain."

"Oh dear, I don't think you will get a wife that way."

"Or I could tell her about the winter mornings when I awake and look out of my window, and the mist is a white veil over everything, so that the castle seems to be floating. Or the summer mornings when the sun is rising over the forest and the birds are just waking and singing their joy for the day ahead. Either way, 'tis a magical sight."

Angus and Selina had wandered off some time ago, so they were alone. He took a peek toward Penelope and found her leaning back against the picnic basket, with an expression on her face he could not quite read. But she was listening, so he carried on.

"On the misty days, it is so quiet that I like to walk into the forest and stop and listen. Sometimes a bird will rustle in the bushes, or I will see the outline of a stag, and he is listening, too. My father does not allow hunting at Bonnyrigg. There used to be, but when he became duke, he stopped it altogether. When he first came to Bonnyrigg and met my mother, he was a gamekeeper, and part of his job was to care for the creatures on the estate. I think I would have made a good gamekeeper, too."

"Don't you want to be a duke?" Her voice was soft, curious.

He stared at the sky a moment more. "No, I never did. I told you how, when I found out I was going to be one, I ran away into the forest and hid. They found me, eventually. I'm still not sure I want to be a duke, but I have become resigned to it. I am the eldest son and the heir, and I will have to step into my father's shoes when the time comes—hopefully that will not be for a long while."

"That is why you need the right wife by your side," Penelope said confidently. "Someone who knows what to do and what to say, and when. She can sit at your dinner table and make conversation, jumping in if there is an awkward pause, smoothing things over if things get heated. And all you would have to do is eat and drink and smile benignly."

"It sounds perfect," he said with a heavy sigh.

"Yes, it does."

Callum closed his eyes. He wanted to look at her. He wanted to say things he knew he could not and which she would put a stop to. He wanted *her*.

He held out his hand, eyes still closed, and said, "Come here, Miss Armstrong, I need your help on a weighty matter."

For a moment he thought she would refuse, or laugh at him, but then he heard the rustle of her clothing and she was at his side, her small hand warm in his.

"What weighty matter?" she said quietly. When he didn't answer at once, she stroked his hair back from his brow, her fingers gentle, and then he felt her lie down beside him, resting her elbow on the blanket so that she could see down into his face. Her breath was warm against his lips.

"I am in need of your kisses," he whispered.

She did not hesitate, but leaned in to kiss him, the lightest brush of her lips against his. He wanted to pull her down and kiss her properly, but it was so sweet that he lay there and let her explore his face with fingers and lips. She nuzzled his closed eyelids, and fluttered her lashes against his.

"Do you like this?" she said. "I used to tease Mortimer when he was a child."

The sadness in her voice struck him to the heart. He did not like to think of her hurt and alone, not ever.

"Do you think he misses you?" he said.

She paused. "I don't know. Every other time we have argued, I have gone to him and begged his forgiveness, even if it was not my fault, but this time . . . I am being strong. He must learn he cannot depend on me for everything and that he must respect me. I think until you spoke of *your* sister, it did not occur to me how little he thinks of my welfare and wellbeing. How selfish he has been for years. I think . . . Uncle Bertie's influence has not been good for him, but I cannot blame my uncle entirely."

"You are right to be strong. There have been occasions when my brother Rory and I have fallen out, and if it weren't for my mother, we would probably never speak to each other again. Rory always believes himself right when he is obviously not. I long, one day, for someone to bring him down a peg or two."

"But he is your brother and you love him," she reminded him softly.

"Aye, but there are times when I do not like him."

Her fingers were tickling his ear, and he reached to catch her hand, lifting it to his mouth. He sucked one finger inside, running his tongue over it, and she caught her breath. He felt the change in the air, the burn of desire, the ache of need. They had made love so many times during the past week, but it was never enough. He always wanted more.

Abruptly, he sat up and gazed around. "Haven't Angus and Selina come back?"

She looked up at him with sleepy eyes, her cheeks flushed. At some point she had let her hair down, and now it fell in soft, silver waves about her face.

"They are still looking at the ruin."

"How long do you think they will be?"

"I'm sure it will be long enough," she said, and smiled.

He lay down on her, his hands already tangling in her hair, and kissed her properly. Soon he was tugging up her skirts, and she arched against him, making breathy sounds, and reached to undo the fastenings on his pantaloons. He was ready—he was always ready for her. And she was ready for him, wrapping her legs around his hips and holding him there. As if he would ever want to escape.

But what had started as another hurried, passionate encounter slowed down until it became something else. His kisses grew slow and deep, while her movements grew languid. She rubbed her cheek against his chest, breathing in his scent, and he smoothed her silky hair and bent to lathe his tongue over her throat.

They knew each other well now, and he was familiar with her gasps and her sighs. Perhaps that was why this was no rushed mating. They took their time joining together, kissing and stroking, not hurrying. And Callum realized that they were making love.

Their climax was long and slow and wonderfully satisfactory. Callum felt it would go on forever, and he wanted it to. If he had ever had any doubts that Penelope was the only woman for him, then they were cast aside forever.

"Have there been many women?" she asked him as they lay quiet, their hands clasped together.

"You'd be amazed how attractive some girls find the shy boy."

She laughed softly. "So that's how you explain it?"

He turned his head and smiled. "I'm not looking for that sort of life. I am not that sort of man. I want one woman to cleave to. And children, I would like children."

For a long time she searched his eyes, seeking to read the secrets in them. He let her. He wanted her to know how he felt. He thought she might say something, share her own longings, but instead she turned away and began to right her clothing.

"I hope you can find that woman," she said lightly, disappointing him. And yet he could tell she meant it. She had a generous heart and she wanted him to succeed and be as happy as it was possible for him to be.

It was not her fault that she had ruined him of that chance by the simple act of being somewhere in the world.

❧❧❧

CHAPTER NINETEEN

ANGUS SIGHED AS he held Selina in his arms, the lichen covered stones of the ruin looming over them. They were both fully clothed, and although they had been kissing, that was as far as it had gone. Now Selina turned her head to look at him, raising her eyebrows. "Whatever is the matter? Are you imagining Cromwell slighting the castle?"

He snorted. "No, I am wondering what I will do when I go home," he said disingenuously. "I am thinking about how lonely I will be without you."

Selina grinned at him. "Oh, is there an alternative to you going home and being lonely?"

He grinned back. "I can kidnap you and ride north with you as my hostage. Does that appeal to you, Selina?"

She thought about it. "I think it does. I have never been kidnapped before, but I am willing to try it."

"It would be something to tell our children."

He felt her go still and then it was Selina who sighed. "I wish I could give you your wish, but I told you before, I'm not sure children are possible at my age, Angus."

Angus, realizing he had said the wrong thing, hurried to reassure her. "I don't need children, Selina. I need you, only you. I'm sorry if I made you think . . ."

She patted the hand that rested around her and leaned her head back on his broad shoulder. "It is all right. I understand. You must find someone younger. I would not have you pining for something that cannot be."

Angus knew he could brush the words aside, go on with their pleasant interlude, but he had realized over the past days that he did not want to live a life without her. Returning to Bonnyrigg without Selina was not to be borne.

"Let me be clear," he said.

She looked up at him with big, worried eyes. "About what?"

"If children are no' possible then I am at peace with that. It is you I want, my love."

"Me?" she squeaked.

"I have lived my life to the full, and I thought I would continue on with that until I was on my deathbed. But I found you, and I know I canna let you go. Will you have me, Selina? Will you marry me? I know it is no' something you can do without considering Miss Armstrong and your life here in London, and you maybe think you are taking a risk. But I am dependable and loyal, and I would treat you verra well."

The truth of his words rang out, and Selina had tears in her eyes as she answered just as seriously. "Thank you, Angus. I want . . . I will have to think on it, but I want to say yes."

He smiled and leaned in to smack his lips against hers.

"There is something more I must tell you," she said, and now she seemed nervous. "My fiancé who died . . . We were waiting for the wedding night to—to be together. And there has been no one since who I trusted enough to allow . . . Well, I am a virgin, Angus. Does that put you off? I understand if you might want a woman with more experience."

He stared and then he laughed. "You think I would refuse you because o' that? Selina, you are giving me a gift! I promise I will be gentle and patient. I have learned much over the years and now I know it was for a reason. It was for you."

He held her close, promising he would love her and show her how much she meant to him.

"How can I leave Penelope?" she said at last, as they were preparing to return to the picnic. They had made certain to give the other couple enough time together. As Angus and Selina were well aware, they would be doing more than taking lessons on etiquette.

Angus wasn't sure how to answer her. He had his own worries when it came to Callum. A brief affair had turned into a problem. He was aware that the lad had fallen head over heels in love. Selina had said she was sure that her mistress felt the same, but Angus did not know Miss Armstrong as well as her maid did.

What hope did they have? Penelope's reputation was in tatters and it was doubtful Maxwell MacKenzie would welcome her into his castle. Angus had noticed he sometimes had strong opinions on the subject of fallen women—a step back into his Calvinist past—and rather hypocritical when you thought about it. Angus thought that Luna would be more likely to agree to a union with Penelope. If Callum was happy, then she would overlook the obstacles. Maxwell . . . well, he was another matter.

And Angus just knew he would be the one who got the blame. He had looked away for just a moment, seen Selina and been distracted. He had misjudged Callum's feelings for Miss Armstrong, and now this was the consequence.

Thank the lord that the lessons would only last another two days and then it would be over. The Countess of Strathmore's ball was fast approaching. Callum would be upset, yes, the lad had a soft heart, but he would just have to learn that not everything had a happy ending. Or at least the ending he wanted. Life was a matter of compromises, Angus told himself, refusing to consider that he was not making one himself when it came to Selina.

Relieved that his problems might soon be over, Angus turned his attention back to his lady love.

CHAPTER TWENTY

ONCE MORE, THEY were in the sitting room at Jasmyne Street. Penelope told herself that tomorrow night Callum would be dancing and showing himself off at his Aunt Jennie's ball. She knew he wasn't looking forward to it. He had already told her that he felt like a roasted bird set upon a dinner table for others to look over and feast upon. She had soothed his anxieties, telling him that he was a handsome, charming gentleman and if anyone thought otherwise, they were not worth his time.

"Someone will want to marry you," she assured him. "Several someones. After tomorrow night, you will have so many invitations you will have difficulty choosing which ones to accept."

He gave her a sideways look. "I find that a wee bit unlikely."

"Do you doubt my ability to turn you from a Highland brute into an eligible gentleman?"

"No, I don't mean that. I may well receive invitations by the bucketload, but they will be of no use to me."

She frowned.

He seemed to be gathering himself, and she had the horrid feeling he was going to say something she did not want to hear. Something that would mean she must tell him to leave, and then sit sobbing alone with her broken heart. Penelope had hoped that she had at least another day with him. One more tryst to store away in her treasured memory box for later.

"Callum—"

He shook his head. "No, I will say what I must. It is pointless me trying to woo one of the ladies I will meet at the ball. Because . . ." He drew himself up. "What if I have already met the lady I want to marry?"

Penelope hoped her face was not as pale as she thought it must be. "Have you?" She tried for a joke. "I hope it isn't one of the ladies you encountered at the Bohemian Ball. What is her name?"

He wasn't amused. He was watching her carefully.

"I hope she is pretty," she babbled on. "Or at least kind and patient."

"She is beautiful," he said quietly. "And clever, kind, and very patient."

Abruptly, she stood up, and her hands were shaking as she clasped them tightly together. "Did you know I have another client after you? He is a sad case, but his mother believes I can get him up to scratch. I had thought my days as a teacher might be done after my brother's behavior in the park. But it seems not! Of course I am very relieved. This is my vocation, you see. I would never willingly give it up."

He was staring at her as if he was having difficulty understanding her.

"So you see I will be perfectly all right," she went on, in case it was his kind heart that was driving him to ask her to marry him. Because that was what this was about. It must be. He was infatuated and he was thoughtful, and now the two had forced him into a proposal that would be disastrous for him.

He seemed to understand her meaning at last. "I see," he said. Before he could say more, Selina entered the room. Penelope shot her a look of desperate relief.

"I was just telling MacKenzie about my new client," she said hurriedly.

"Oh, yes," Selina nodded, but she looked startled.

Penelope began fussing about the state of the cushions on the settee and asking Selina what cake she would bake for this new client, the fictitious client that didn't exist. Callum had slowly risen to his own feet and stood, watching her in silence. She glanced at him once or twice but could no longer guess what he was thinking. He had turned his head and was staring out of the window.

"I think we will end your lessons here, Callum," she said at last, her smile bright and hard, and her heart rattling painfully in her chest. "There is nothing more I can teach you. Congratulations on becoming the perfect gentleman."

He nodded. "Of course," he said in a voice that was strangely devoid of feeling. "And thank you, Miss Armstrong, for all you have done to help me. I will never . . . I will not forget you."

Penelope curtsied to his bow. It was a very nice bow. She should be proud of her part in that bow. It was a pity she could feel nothing but grief.

He left, the door closing behind him, Selina following him down the stairs. She could hear their voices fading, and then silence. He was gone.

Good, she thought. There had never been any chance of a happy ending between them, and he must have known that just as she did. And she wouldn't cry, at least not until she was alone.

Selina had returned and was watching her with sympathy. "Are you sure—" she began.

"Very sure. Give me a moment. I need to—to . . ."

A tear ran down her cheek but she wiped it quickly away. Not now. Soon her lies would come true, and she would have a new client to prepare for and she must not fail. Callum would become one of her brightest successes, and word would spread. It *must*.

And if it didn't? Just for an instant she imagined making that awful step back into the past and throwing herself onto the mistress market. Lord Freith would welcome her with open arms.

She shuddered.

"My dear Penelope," Selina said gently. "You are making a mistake."

Penelope shook her head wildly, no longer able to stop the

tears. "No, I am preventing *him* from making a mistake. We would both be so dreadfully unhappy."

Selina took her in her arms and held her tight, letting her weep, not saying a word. Penelope was glad of that. She didn't want to hear any more arguments. Her head was already aching with them, and she had made her decision.

It was over, and she *must* move on.

OUTSIDE THE HOUSE in Jasmyne Street, Callum had come to a stop. He wasn't sure what to think. He had obviously messed up what he had planned to say, which was that he had already met the woman he wanted to marry and it was Penelope. Somehow she had turned it around. And then before he could gather his wits, she had begun talking about this new client and how much she enjoyed her—her vocation. After that, he hadn't felt able to say the words burning a hole in his tongue.

He stood on the doorstep, wondering if he should go back inside and start again. But what was the point? She had dismissed him, and he would only embarrass them both by persisting.

As for this new client . . . he had never hated anyone more.

Unless it was Mortimer.

Just then, someone cleared their throat and Callum looked up at whoever was standing on the street.

For a moment, he couldn't believe his eyes. Mortimer was standing there. It *was* Mortimer, wasn't it? He looked far younger than Callum remembered, and the expression on his face suggested he was very unsure of his welcome. His gaze slid uneasily by Callum to the front door, and then back again.

"Is my sister in?" he asked.

"Why? Are you going to insult her again?" Callum growled. "She doesn't want to see you."

Mortimer stared down at his boots. "What I said . . . I'm

sorry," he said in a miserable voice. "I was hoping to make amends, but perhaps it is too late." He looked up, and his eyes were moist with tears. "Do you think it's too late?"

Callum watched him in silence, his blistering words drying up in his throat. Had the boy grown a conscience? Something certainly seemed to have happened to change his manner from their previous encounter.

"Uncle Bertie has decided I need to move out," he went on awkwardly, answering *that* question. "Without Pen's funds, he can't afford me, and he's found a new partner to help finance the invention."

"Is that what this is then?" Callum said angrily. "You need somewhere to stay, and you thought that your sister would forgive you and take you in."

Mortimer shuffled uneasily. "It's not just that. I *am* sorry for what I said. I've been a selfish little boy, and when Bertie told me I had to go, I—I realized how stupid and mercenary I had been. Last night I lay awake remembering everything that Penelope has done for me, how ungrateful I have been, and realizing that if she refuses to speak to me then I will be quite . . ." His voice cracked.

"Alone," Callum guessed. "Poor you."

Mortimer's eyes sparked briefly with anger before they dulled again. "Yes. I don't want to blame anyone but myself, but Uncle Bertie made me feel important. Like I was doing something that mattered. And now I know I wasn't. It was just a silly invention that no one will want, and because of my own stupidity, I've probably lost the one person who has always loved me."

Callum wished this encounter hadn't happened now—he really did not have the patience for it. But if he could help Penelope and her brother reconcile, surely he had to do it?

"She'll forgive you," he said brusquely. "Apologize and explain what an idiot you've been. She loves you too much not to take you back."

Hope flared in Mortimer's eyes, so much like his sister's. "Do you really think so?"

Callum couldn't help but smile. "I do."

Mortimer nodded and climbed the steps and went to step around him, only to stop again and ask curiously, "What are you doing here? Are you still having lessons on etiquette?"

Callum shook his head brusquely, ignoring the pang in his chest. "We are done with that. I have finished. I was hoping . . ." He stopped himself. What business of Mortimer's were his private wishes and dreams? "Never mind. Go and see your sister."

Mortimer hesitated a moment as if he knew there was more to learn behind Callum's glum face, and then he reached to rattle the door knocker.

Callum walked away, leaving behind him the house in Jasmyne Street. He had done Penelope a good deed and his conscience was clear. And if he never saw her again . . .

Best not to think about that. The ball was tomorrow night, and perhaps he could call in and tell her how it went? But no, she would not like that. She had said her goodbyes and wished him well. Whatever his own feelings, hers had been clear.

It was over.

CHAPTER TWENTY-ONE

Selina had stood in the entry to the house for far longer than Mortimer had expected, barring his way, until he finally convinced her to let him in. He should have been angry, but he couldn't manage it, not when he remembered what he had said to Penelope. Selina was just protecting her, as any good friend should. She was a better friend to his sister than he had ever been.

It was time to humble himself, to apologize, and he did.

"I have come to beg my sister's forgiveness," he said, meeting Selina's eyes directly. "I am very sorry for what I said and did. Please let me speak to her."

She looked startled, and then not sure if she believed him or not.

"Please," he repeated.

Maybe it was his expression or the tears in his eyes, but Selina nodded and stepped aside. "She is upset right now. Not about you," she added quickly. "But she needs her brother. Don't disappoint me," she added in a harsh whisper.

As he climbed the stairs to the sitting room, Mortimer told himself he could be the brother he should have been for all these years. He could show Penelope that he was a changed man. He opened the door.

She was seated, and her head was bent into her hands. She was crying! At first Mortimer was shocked—he could not remember the last time he had seen her cry. His first instinct was to turn and run—he had never been very good at dealing with painful emotions—but then he was ashamed of himself. This was not the time to fall at the first hurdle. If Pen was going to forgive him, then he needed to start acting like her devoted brother.

"Pen?"

She startled and dropped her hands, turning to him. He could see her face was blotched and her eyes red, before she hastily looked away, pretending to straighten some cushions.

"M-Mortimer! My goodness. What are you doing here?"

He didn't bother answering. Instead, he hurried over to her and dropped to his knees at her feet. Just for a moment he was reminded of doing something like this when he was a child, gazing up at her like she was everything to him and as if there was nothing bad she could not mend. The memory made him feel a little sick when he thought he might have lost his sister forever.

Her face was still turned away, and he took her hands in his, feeling how chilled they were. In fact, the whole room was chilly. Was she economizing on coal again? He glanced over to the hearth and saw the scuttle was empty. She used to do this years ago, whenever she was worried their pennies would not stretch far enough.

"Pen, I am here to apologize. I am so sorry. I was an oaf. A selfish, horrible oaf. Like the goblin in that story you used to read to me. Do you remember? Please forgive me."

She looked at him and managed a wobbly smile. "I do remember, and of course I forgive you."

"I am so glad," he said with obvious relief. "The things I said to you . . . I don't think I could live with myself if you didn't forgive me, Pen."

She squeezed his hands. "Well, I do. What has happened?" she added, searching his face for clues. "What has Uncle Bertie done?"

He longed to tell her about Bertie and his heartless behavior, but he hesitated. Penelope probably already knew what their uncle was like. She had been trying to warn him about it for years. So instead of moaning about his own bad fortune, he said, "What has happened to make you cry? That Scots brute was outside just now. What has he done to you?" he added, ready to set off back down the stairs and challenge the fellow to a duel. No matter how big he was.

But Pen shook her head. "It's not his fault," she said gloomily. "I forgot my most important rule when it comes to clients and allowed myself to—to fall in love. Don't worry, I will get over it." She nodded jerkily and added in a determined voice, "I have to, despite feeling so wretched. I am so glad you're here, Mortimer."

Mortimer remembered the look on the brute's face and thought he hadn't appeared to be very happy either. Was this a case of star-crossed lovers? Or a serious misunderstanding?

He got up from his uncomfortable position on the hard floor and sat down beside his sister. "Do you want me to punch him for you?" he asked seriously. "I've been practicing since the last time. I go to a boxing club one day a week."

She stared, and then she gave a choked chuckle. "No, no violence today," she said. "Let's eat cake instead. Selina!"

Selina must have been waiting outside the door because she answered at once. She gave Penelope a thorough examination, and whatever she saw must have satisfied her doubts. She smiled, and then smiled at Mortimer, too.

"Well now," she said, "I have orange cake or seed cake, which is it to be?"

"Both!" they shouted and then fell about laughing as if they were children again.

SELINA WAS SMILING as she went to fetch the cake. She was so glad that Mortimer had apologized, and Penelope had her brother back again. It would make it much easier for her to take up Angus's offer and leave with him.

She stopped. Was she really considering abandoning her friend? How could she walk away after all this time? They had so many memories between them, good and bad. Could she really be so selfish as to put her own pleasure first?

And yet Selina reminded herself that this might be her last chance to find the sort of happiness that was denied her when her fiancé was killed. And it wasn't like she was clutching at Angus because she saw him as her last chance. She loved him. He was big and strong and forceful, but he was also gentle when it mattered. She had no fear of lying down with him in their marriage bed, and if there were to be children . . . probably not. She didn't expect there to be, but she rather thought that having Angus at her side would be enough.

She could see no regrets in throwing in her lot with him.

Apart from leaving Penelope.

She would have to tell her, and soon. Not right now perhaps, but once the ball was over tomorrow night and Callum MacKenzie had begun the process of choosing his wife.

Why hadn't Penelope been brave enough to marry Callum? Selina knew he wanted her to, and had probably been about to propose when Penelope made up her story about a new client and everything being rosy. Which was why she had been sobbing.

Surely it was worth Penelope taking a chance. But all she could see were the thunderclouds ahead, and none of the sunshine.

Selina arranged the slices of cake to her satisfaction and was about to carry the plate through to the sitting room when the door knocker sounded.

She clicked her tongue, and leaving the food, hurried back down the stairs. Perhaps it was Angus, she thought, her spirits brightening. But it was not Angus. It was a servant holding a message.

"Is this the residence of Miss Armstrong?" he asked in the sort of voice Selina always thought put on.

"It is. What do you want?"

He looked taken aback at her plain speaking and held out a thick, cream envelope. "My mistress wishes her to have this."

By the time Selina looked up from the sender's address—Lady Agatha Hamlyn—the servant was gone. She carried the envelope and the cake into the sitting room.

"This came for you," she said, handing the impressive looking object over to Penelope.

It didn't take her long to read, and when she was finished, she looked up at Mortimer and Serina, her eyes blank. She swallowed. "I don't know whether to be relieved or angry," she said. "Shall I read it to you both?"

She didn't wait for an answer.

Dear Miss Armstrong,

My son is in need of the services of someone who can teach him proper behavior for a young man entering Society. He was brought up in the depths of the country and has no idea how to comport himself. I have asked my acquaintances for the name of an appropriate person, and they speak of you as the only one they believe up to the task. I am fully aware of your unfortunate reputation, and the idea of contact between you and my son is repugnant to me. And yet I feel I have no option if my son is to flourish in the world he was born to. Please visit me at your nearest convenience so that we can discuss the matter.

Lady Agatha Hamlyn

"Well!" Selina said, wanting to snatch the nasty letter back and throw it in the fire—although Penelope's economizing meant that was nothing more than a faint flicker.

She was glad to see that hearing Lady Hamlyn's letter had turned Mortimer's cheeks pink with righteous anger on his sister's behalf.

"How dare she!" he declared. "Tell her no. On second thoughts, throw it away and don't answer. She doesn't deserve your civility."

Penelope gave a little laugh that was more like a hiccup. "And what then?" she asked wearily. "I need her. I need the money she will pay me when I have remodeled her son into the perfect gentleman and ladies are flocking to him. That is what she wants and I can do it."

"But Pen . . ." he gasped.

"What is the alternative?" she interrupted.

He opened his mouth, closed it again. "I am so sorry, Pen," he whispered.

The next moment they were hugging, and Selina wiped a tear from her eye. There was an alternative, and she longed to voice it, but Penelope would refuse to listen. She set down the cake and left them to their emotional reunion.

CHAPTER TWENTY-TWO

CALLUM LOOKED ABOUT him at Aunt Jennie's ballroom. It was decorated with flowers and greenery, candles glowed, and everything that could be polished was. His aunt had hired an orchestra that looked very professional, and there was a table groaning with more than enough food to keep the guests sustained for the hours to come.

There were also ladies young and old, whispering behind their fans, their eyes bright with anticipation. Most of them seemed to be focused on him.

Callum should have felt uncomfortable, certainly nervous, but he found he wasn't. Penelope's lessons had prepared him well for the task ahead. His aunt had complimented him on his clothing, and his uncle's valet had him looking "ship-shape". What could possibly go wrong? Apart from another mouse, he supposed. That made him smile, remembering the Bohemian Ball and the hysterics of the guests. Penelope had laughed and then they had made love, and . . .

He shut out the memories.

Callum had promised himself he would do his best tonight. He would try to please his aunt and fulfill his father's dream for him and make him proud, he really would.

He looked about him again, trying to see someone who caused him a modicum of interest, but all the ladies looked the same. Not the same in a physical way. They were tall and short and middling, fair haired and dark haired, pretty and plain. No doubt there were several among them worthy of his attentions, and who would please Maxwell if he brought them home.

But none of them were Penelope, and that was the problem.

It took Callum an hour of dancing and chatting and being pleasant—so very pleasant it made his teeth ache—to acknowledge that he would never find the woman of his dreams in this room. He longed for the sort of conversations he had with Penelope, where she told him what he was doing wrong in that high-handed voice. He so wanted to hear her lectures. None of the guests here tonight dared to speak to him like that, they were all so polite.

It was as if the boar incident had never happened, nor the brawl in the park. Somehow that was all forgotten, and he wondered what his aunt had said to make it so. Reminded them of his title perhaps, and his wealth, and his estate in Scotland.

"You are not at all as I expected," one of the ladies blurted out when he bowed to her after their dance.

"What did you expect?" he inquired courteously.

She giggled nervously. "I was told you were ill-mannered, but I can see you are not." Then, realizing what she had said, "I do beg your pardon, my lord." Her eyes were very big, and she seemed very young, so he forgave her.

"Are you sure you are the Marquess of Morven?" another lady spluttered as he escorted her to the supper table.

"Unless there are two of us," Callum said politely.

"Yes," the woman spoke with relief, "that must be it. I am thinking of the *other* one."

It was just too ridiculous for words, and he had had enough. How many times could one discuss the weather—Penelope had been right, it was the main topic of conversation—or which social events were the ones to be seen at. Or the latest juicy gossip. Having been the subject of gossip, Callum was not eager to join in tearing to shreds some other poor unfortunate.

He wanted to leave. He appreciated his aunt's efforts, but he could see by her glances in his direction that she was aware he wasn't enjoying himself. She knew him too well. He was sorry she had gone to so much trouble, but he couldn't help it. He wanted to go home, and he wanted to take Penelope with him. He wanted to marry her first, of course, and then face his father, and if Maxwell didn't like his choice of wife then it was just too bad.

They would find somewhere else to live. He would be a duke one day, but until then they could roam about, living their lives to the full, and being *happy*. Because after tonight, he knew for certain he could never be happy with anyone but Penelope Armstrong.

But Callum loved his Aunt Jennie, so he forced himself to stay and do his duty until the ball was over and the guests had left. Then he sat in the library, mulling over his thoughts, and drank a glass of whisky brought to him by a stone-faced Hocking. And only then did he go to find her.

Jennie was in her bedchamber, lying back on a mountain of pillows with a cup of hot chocolate and Bothwell perched on her lap. The cat gave him a disgusted look—no doubt he knew about the mouse that had been denied him—but Callum ignored the monster.

Jennie startled at the sight of him and set her cup down with a clatter on its saucer. "Callum?"

"Aunt Jennie," he said, and took a breath before launching into his speech. "Thank you for tonight. I am very grateful. And for the lessons—I am sure I am a better man for them. You have done everything you could to help me find the wife my father wants for me, and I believe in my heart that I have done all I can to grant him his wish."

Jennie raised an eyebrow. "But?" She sounded resigned.

He sat down on the edge of the bed, much to Bothwell's disgust. "*But* it's of no use. I am in love, and I can't just pretend otherwise. I can't marry someone else when I want her. It would be callous to my wife and myself."

Jennie reached out to stroke the cat. Bothwell began to purr, at the same time giving Callum a sour look. "I presume you mean Penelope Armstrong," she said, with no surprise. "I should have seen the way things were heading and put a stop to it."

"I don't think you could have. It was instant, and my feelings have only grown from there."

She looked up at him, so like his mother despite their different coloring, it made his heart ache even more for home. "What will Maxwell say?"

Callum ran a hand through his hair and gave it a tug. He missed running his hands through his wild curls, and he determined to let it grow again now he no longer had to pretend to be a gentleman.

"I don't know what my father will say. I intend to write to him tonight. I will tell him that I am going to ask Penelope to marry me, and if she does, I will bring her home to Bonnyrigg. If he wishes to banish us, then I will find somewhere else to live. I have my allowance from my grandfather. I am not a poor man."

"*If* she will marry you?" Jennie sat up straighter. "Is there a question about that?"

"She says she will not, that she is not the wife I need. She is selfless like that. I intend to convince her she is wrong, but . . ." He didn't want to think what it would mean if she rejected him. "Either way, I am going home to Bonnyrigg. I don't belong here."

"I think tonight you did a very good job of belonging," she retorted. "If you gave yourself a little longer, you might discover it is not so bad. Let me arrange some more social events, redirect your thoughts to other—"

"It would be no use," he said gently. "Thank you for all you have done for me. I am sorry to disappoint you. I canna help the way I feel."

She waved an impatient hand. "You must follow your heart, Callum. I truly believe that. And your heart is at Bonnyrigg and, it seems, with Miss Armstrong. I wish you luck. If things don't go to plan, if Maxwell . . . You always have a home here with me."

He was moved beyond speaking. He reached out and took

her hand in his, much to Bothwell's ire. "Thank you, Aunt Jennie. I promise to visit and I hope you will visit me."

In his own bedchamber, Callum sat down with pen and paper and began his letter to his father. It was probably too long and rather rambling, but it was honest and heartfelt. When he was done, he read over it and was as happy as he could be. If Maxwell did not want to listen to his eldest son's outpourings then it was too bad. Callum would be very sorry to fall out with a man he had always loved and admired, but he was willing to take that risk for the sake of the woman he adored.

And what if Penelope refused to marry him, which was a real possibility?

Callum wasn't sure what he would do then. He couldn't think beyond it. Some part of his heart was telling him that she loved him too, and he preferred to listen to that.

CHAPTER TWENTY-THREE

P ENELOPE SAT DOWN to breakfast and poured herself a cup of coffee. Mortimer greeted her with, "Did you reply to that awful woman's letter?"

She had written a polite reply to Lady Hamlyn, thanking her for her interest and offering some of the strategies she might use with the woman's son. She was pleased with the result, but whether Lady Hamlyn would be pleased remained to be seen. She told herself she was relieved that she was being given another chance and tried to set aside her worries. Foolishly, Penelope had thought herself secure in her employment, but she now knew she was anything but.

It felt like she had been strolling along, oblivious to everything, and had fallen into a deep hole in the ground. It was dark and cold, and somehow she had to claw her way out again. But even if she did reach the top and was able to drag herself back to solid ground, that did not mean she was safe. It might only be a matter of time before she fell again.

Mortimer was waiting for her answer and she tried to sound cheerful.

"Yes, I have replied, Mortimer. The letter is on the hall table ready to be posted."

He eyed her rather anxiously. She knew she looked dreadful. She hadn't slept and had spent the night thinking about Callum at his aunt's ball and all the pretty young things who would be fluttering about him, seeking his attention. Perhaps he had already chosen his future wife from among them. Someone suitable, who would win his heart and make him happy. Or at least make his father happy.

She took a shaky breath and sipped at her coffee, telling herself to stop it. The time for regrets was over. She could never have married him and ruined his future, they both knew that. He could move on now, put aside their mad affair, and so must she.

Mortimer spread butter and jam on his toast and bit into it with relish. Penelope smiled to herself. At least she had her brother back. Uncle Bertie had burned his bridges there, and Mortimer had finally seen the light. He was apologetic and almost a changed boy, but she suspected he would never change completely. They would be at odds again at some point, but for now she was very grateful.

The knocker clattered on the door downstairs.

Penelope looked at the clock and frowned. It was far too early for visitors. Perhaps Lady Hamlyn had sent another of her charming letters? Perhaps she had changed her mind? She pushed that thought aside before it could send her deeper into the hole.

"Why doesn't Selina answer the door?" Mortimer asked, finishing off his toast.

"She went to the shops. She likes to get the best cuts of meat for the lowest price. I'll get it."

But before Penelope could rise to her feet, Mortimer did so.

"I'll go," he said cheerfully. "And if it is another one of those hateful letters, I will send it back."

"No, Mortimer!" she called out as he left the room.

She heard the door open and voices downstairs. It sounded as if her brother exclaimed, "Oh, thank God!" which surprised her, and then there were two sets of footsteps coming back up the stairs toward her.

She fumbled with her napkin. Perhaps she was having a premonition. Or this was a dream. Because she recognized those footsteps.

Callum.

She tried to tell herself that if it was him then he was only coming to tell her how well the evening had gone and he had made his choice, and to say goodbye. Yet some small, ridiculous part of her whispered that maybe he had come for her.

"Pen, look who's here!" Mortimer said in a jolly voice as Callum entered the room. He took note of his sister's face and added, "I'll leave you to it then."

She wanted to tell him to stay, but the words seemed to be jammed in her throat. Instead, she said, "MacKenzie," in a voice that didn't sound like her own.

He closed the door and came into the room. He looked pale but resolute, as if he had a mission and was going to carry it out no matter what. She stood up and gestured with a shaky hand toward the couch near the fireplace. There was no fire—she was still saving on coal.

"Please, sit down. Would you like some tea? Coffee? I'm sorry Selina isn't here to make you fresh."

"I don't want tea or coffee," he said rudely, and then corrected himself. "I don't want tea or coffee, *thank you*."

She sat down abruptly. He sounded as if something had happened. It must be that he had chosen a wife. Already! Her heart sank, but she reminded herself that of course he was in demand. Impossible that he was not. A man like Callum.

"I have a request for you," he said, still standing and gazing down at her.

"Oh?" Her neck was hurting from staring up at him.

"I want another lesson. I need to know how to propose."

Her mind went momentarily blank. "Propose? Oh, yes. Oh, of course. Then you have . . ." She stopped herself from continuing with that thought. Best not to know, at least until she could pretend to be happy for him. Right now her emotions were so raw, she would fail miserably.

"I know the basics," he said, watching her closely, "but I think there is more to it."

"Yes." She cleared her throat and told herself to stop this

hysterical nonsense. She could cry when he had gone, although surely to goodness she had cried enough recently. "Usually the gentleman kneels."

"Right. Ah, both knees?"

"No, traditionally it is the left knee. Oh. Are you practicing?" She stared as he went down on his left knee before her. "Yes, like that. And then you take the lady's hand in yours and say your piece. Although you should have requested an audience with her father or guardian first. There's no use proposing if he is going to refuse you permission."

He waited and then said, "Have you finished blathering?"

Her eyes widened. "MacKenzie, that is no way to speak to a lady! Try again."

"Will you marry me, Penelope?"

She stilled and then took a shaky breath. "Very good, but perhaps use the name of the woman whose hand you are actually asking for. Try again."

He cleared his throat, and there was a glint in his eyes that confused her. "Will you marry me, Penelope, and live with me at Bonnyrigg, and be my love forevermore?"

"You—you . . ."

His serious expression lightened into an almost smile. "And what if she has no father or guardian? Just a rather irritating brother. Should I ask him?"

It occurred to her after a moment that he might mean Mortimer, but if so then she must not allow this to happen. "Callum—" she began hurriedly, meaning to stop him.

"I don't care what you say," he said, and took her hands firmly in his. She tried to tug them free, but he refused to let them go. It was ridiculous, and in other circumstances she might have laughed.

"Callum, please!"

"No, I will propose to you whether you like it or not. Penelope, will you marry me? I love you and I cannot imagine myself with any other woman. I have written to my father and told him I will have you or no one else, and if he wants to banish me then he can. I have funds of my own, so we can live comfortably enough. Have I covered everything? I think so." His voice dropped into a lower key with a husky note, raising the hairs on the back of her neck. "Please marry me, Penelope."

She blinked. "I will ruin you," she said. "What of my reputation?"

"You won't. You are perfect. While I am out strolling in my forests, you can run my castle and take tea with my neighbors. The thought of all that socializing makes me shudder, but I know you love it. Can't you see you are the one for me? I canna imagine being with anyone else. I would not want to."

"Callum," she wailed, but the strange thing was those low spirits she had been dealing with were beginning to rise. It was almost like a wedge of sunlight had penetrated into that dark hole she had imagined herself crouched in, and if she lifted her face, she could feel its warmth.

"I am asking you to marry me," he said patiently. "Give me your answer, Penelope. Forget about everything and everyone else. Think of yourself for a change, and me. Think of us together. What is your answer?"

There was only one answer. Tears ran down her cheeks. "Yes," she said. "Yes, please!"

He closed his eyes in relief, and then he was grinning and reaching for her, and she was in his arms. "Thank God," he muttered into her hair. "Imagine my embarrassment if I arrived home without you, after that bloody letter to my father."

She managed to laugh. "I had a letter about a new client," she said, probably blathering again. "It was horrible. She made it sound like I was being hired *despite* all of my shortcomings."

"I thought you already had a new client," he said, leaning back to look into her face.

"I—I lied," she admitted. "Because I didn't want you to ruin your life by declaring yourself to me."

He gave her a little shake. "Ruin it? You have completed my

life, Penelope. Don't you know that? I love you so much, so, so much."

"I love you, too," she whispered. "Callum, so much."

They might have said more, but they were interrupted by whooping and cheering from outside the door. The next moment it was flung open, and Mortimer and Selina came rushing in, faces flushed with joy, both of them hugging each other, and then Penelope and Callum.

Penelope wasn't sure if them being so happy was a good thing. "He hasn't saved me," she said, when she was able to get a word in. "He hasn't rescued me. I was quite capable of saving myself. I had a new client and—"

"I'm not saving you!" Callum replied loudly. "Well, I suppose I am. But you are saving me, too. From a miserable marriage with a woman I do not love, or else spending the rest of my days alone in the forest, wishing you were there."

Penelope was moved beyond speech, so it was just as well Selina spoke for her.

"Let us just say you saved each other," she said gently.

CHAPTER TWENTY-FOUR

THE REST OF the morning felt like a dream to Callum. They spoke of their plans, and then Angus arrived—Selina had sent for him—and Callum learned that the two of them had planned to go north to Bonnyrigg and start their own married lives. Callum was surprised and pleased, especially because it would mean Penelope would have her friend with her.

"I really am glad for you," Mortimer said, although he looked a little down in the mouth. "That awful Lady Hamlyn. Can I write her a reply and tell her to go and jump?"

"As much as I would like to do that—" his sister began.

"It's a deal then." Mortimer rubbed his hands together, but then his excitement dropped away. "I'll miss you, Pen."

"You can come with us," Callum said, before he could stop himself. The boy had only just reconciled with his sister and now they were to be parted again, so it was only fair he make the offer.

Mortimer shot him a doubtful look. "Thank you, but I'm not sure that Scotland is the place for me. I will visit, of course I will, but I think London is where I am most comfortable. Can I stay here in Jasmyne Street? For the time being at least."

"Of course you can. But Mortimer, how will you afford to live here? Please tell me you won't be asking Uncle Bertie for help?"

"No, I am done with Uncle Bertie," Mortimer said cheerfully. "I have had an offer from someone else who wants me to be their secretary. I have a reasonable hand and can spell, and I think that is all that is required."

"Secretary?" Penelope blinked. "From whom, Mortimer?"

Her brother looked uncomfortable. "Lord Muir's son. Do you remember him? Sometimes Lord Muir would bring him to Chelsea, while he and you . . ." He coughed. "He remembered me, and I think he was embarrassed about his father's selfishness and that was why he has come to me with the offer. I thought about turning him down, and I will if you want me to. If it is too awkward."

Penelope thought a moment. Lord Muir's son had turned out to be far more generous than his father. "No, don't turn him down," she said quickly. "I feel no animosity toward him or his father. That is in the past." She looked at Callum, worried what he might think.

"I am more interested in the future," he said firmly.

Selina had brought in tea and more cake and now she sat beside Angus. "So are we," she said.

"I thought we could handfast at the border," Angus added, smiling at his lady love.

Penelope looked puzzled. "You mean like Gretna Green?"

"Aye. We will join hands before the blacksmith and two witnesses, and swear to live the rest of our lives together. 'Tis as good a marriage as any."

Callum could see that Penelope was less than thrilled about that. "We will marry from my aunt's house," he said soothingly. "I'll get a license." He wanted everything to be legal under British law, no loopholes that might cause questions and doubts in the future.

"Shouldn't you wait until your father answers your letter?" Penelope said.

"No," Callum replied gruffly. "I have told him what I am doing, and if he doesn't like it then too bad."

Angus snorted a laugh. "You sound just like him," he said. Then, "I remember when the MacKenzies returned to Bonnyrigg to fulfil their promise to the old duke. Callum here decided he didn't like his new life and ran away. Maxwell found him after several days of searching. The boy had made his home in a tree."

There was laughter, but Callum remembered it painfully well. "I didn't want to be a duke," he said. "I wondered why I had to. Why I couldn't do what I wanted, which was to live in a tree."

Angus continued the story. "And Maxwell said, 'Because you can't!'"

Callum smiled. "And I insisted, 'Why?' and I was almost in tears. I was fourteen but still a wee boy inside."

"Aye, you had a gentle heart," Angus said fondly. "You were also verra stubborn."

"And my father sighed and said, 'I made a promise to return to Bonnyrigg. It was part of the deal when I married your mother, and I wanted to marry her above all else, Callum. You will understand one day, when you love a woman so much that you will sacrifice everything to be with her.'"

When he finished, there was silence, and he smiled at Penelope. "I understand now. And I understand that it doesn't feel like a sacrifice because you are what I want, with or without Bonnyrigg."

WHEN THE TIME for Callum and Penelope's marriage arrived, there was still no reply from Maxwell, nor any sign of one. Callum could only assume his father was extremely disappointed and displeased and would inform him of it when he saw him. It did not matter. Well, it did, but he would not allow it to spoil his wedding day.

Aunt Jennie had arranged for a small gathering after the ceremony, and everyone was very merry. She reminisced about the old days at Bonnyrigg and they drank a toast to the days to come.

Afterward, in his bedchamber, Callum held Penelope in his arms. They had waited until this day to lie together again, and the waiting had been agony. His desire for her had not gone away, and judging by her eagerness to get him undressed, neither had hers.

They were to set off in the morning, with Angus and Selina, for the long journey north. Callum was looking forward to it, but he suspected Penelope was developing a bad case of nerves. She was sacrificing more than he was, he understood that, and he was very grateful, but if his father did not welcome them, then he had already decided they would ride on immediately to Inverness and take lodgings there.

Penelope seemed to think it was Callum who was worrying. "I wish you would stop frowning," she said, and leaned over to kiss him. "Whatever happens, we will make our own happiness."

"Of course we will." He kissed her back, gently, and then with more passion.

She groaned and pressed against him. "You are like my favorite dessert, and I want a second helping. Or a third."

He grinned in delight. "Raspberry syllabub?"

"Exactly. When you spilled it on your shirt, and then licked it off your chest. For goodness sake, Callum, I wanted to join in."

He kissed her again, feeling himself already hard at the thought. He had planned several trysts around the estate at Bonnyrigg, and in various corners of the castle where they would not be discovered.

She pushed against his chest and, when he rolled over, climbed upon him like a naked goddess. He cupped her breasts, tweaking at her nipples, and helped her to arrange herself over him. As she pressed down, and he filled her, Callum said some words it was just as well she did not understand. She would not approve, but he could not help it, because it was so good. It was always so good.

She scraped her nails across his belly and he groaned again, arching up. "Temptress," he said.

"But you are so tempting," she whispered.

He met her eyes and suddenly it was as if the moment went

on forever, as if they were under a spell. He remembered again the stories his father had told, of the fairies who lured travelers to their magical abode and kept them there forever.

And then she was riding him and he forgot everything else in the exquisite pleasure. How could he have been so lucky as to marry this woman? Who would have thought, when he rode south to London, that he would be going to meet his destiny in the shape of a petite beauty with silver eyes and moonlight hair? A woman with a sharp tongue that made him ache to claim her, and hold onto her forevermore.

CHAPTER TWENTY-FIVE

THE JOURNEY FROM London to Scotland was long. There was no doubt Penelope had left behind the mellow countryside of her home and entered a far wilder and less civilized realm, and with every day that passed, she felt her fears grow. Callum was attentive, ensuring they had the most comfortable rooms in the most comfortable inns, and she tried her best to hide her anxiety. She had made her bed now, as the saying went, and must lie in it. And lying in bed with Callum was one of her favorite things. The closer they got to his home, the more her husband spoke of it and his family, and Penelope was in no doubt of his love for both. She did not want to come between them, and she did not want him to have to choose.

"Dinna fash, my love," he whispered to her the final night before their arrival at the castle. "We will muddle through it."

"Yes," she agreed with a confidence she wasn't feeling. "Of course we will."

Penelope had been expecting Bonnyrigg to be grand, but it was more than that. A castle fit for a duke, set in one of the wilder parts of Scotland. Mountains rose to the rear of the turreted building, their snow caps seeming close enough to touch, while the forest cradled the castle on three sides. There was something very untamed about it that spoke to her despite her growing worries about her reception.

When their coach arrived at the front door, there were people standing, waiting for them. Callum held her hand, and she wanted to cling to him, but now the moment to face his family had come, she knew she must not show weakness. She suspected Maxwell would despise her if she simpered and begged to be liked.

She had been told that Callum resembled his father to a marked degree, and now she saw that was the truth. Tall and handsome, dark hair streaked with some grey, and brown eyes, he was how Callum would look in years to come. His mother Luna was smaller, with flaming red hair and bright, watchful blue eyes. It was Luna who came forward and took Penelope's hands to rise her from her curtsy.

"My dear," she said, her voice husky with emotion, "you are just as my sister described you. Welcome! Welcome to Bonnyrigg."

That was certainly more kindness than she had expected, and she blinked away sudden tears, while behind her she heard Callum's sigh of relief. "Thank you," she said quietly. "I am grateful to be here."

She wanted to say that she understood this was not what Callum's parents had hoped for, she wanted to explain, but this was not the time. Besides, the rest of Callum's family were descending upon her.

"I am Rory. How do you do?" The man with red hair like his mother's spoke in a low, confident voice. He slid his gaze over her in a practiced gesture as he took her hand. "Callum is a lucky laddie."

Callum grunted a warning. "She's mine, brother."

Rory laughed easily, sure of his charms, and moved aside for the other brother, Donal, who looked more like Callum. He also took her hand and smiled sweetly. "Welcome, sister," he said, and again Penelope felt the sting of tears.

"Thank you," she said. "I hope . . . that is, I will do my very best to . . ."

Callum put his arm about her. "You always do your very best," he said firmly. "And here is my sister, Catriona, although we call her Cat."

Cat had their mother's red hair and bright, watchful eyes, but her smile was as sweet as Donal's. "I am so glad you are here," she said, with a sly glance toward her father. "I have longed for a sister. Just think what fun we will have."

Penelope smiled back, but by now she was feeling very overwhelmed.

"Not too much fun," Callum warned, but he spoke indulgently, as one who would endure a great deal from his sister before he lost his temper.

There was a pause, and that was when Maxwell spoke. "Welcome, Callum's wife," he said, but there was no warmth in his voice. "We have made ready a room for your stay."

Everyone seemed to freeze, and glances were exchanged. "Callum's wife" was bad enough, but "for your stay" had an ominous feel to it.

"Stay for as long as you like," Luna added quickly, but that only made it worse.

"Did you receive my letter, Father?" Callum asked, fixing Maxwell with a determined look.

"Aye, I got it," Maxwell said dourly, turning away.

Callum took her hand firmly in his, squeezing her fingers almost painfully, trying to make up for his father's unfriendliness, and walked by her side into the castle that would one day be his.

Penelope tried to take in her surroundings. They were grand in a medieval way, and as her new husband had warned, it was cold. A fire was roaring in what she guessed was the great hall, and then they were climbing the staircase with portraits gazing at her, as unfriendly as Maxwell, and she found herself in a bedchamber with windows overlooking the forest. The fire was lit here, too, and she went to warm her hands.

They were trembling, which annoyed her. She had known this first meeting would be awkward. She would have to work hard to gain acceptance, and she must accede that maybe she never would. You could not force people to like you. Perhaps they would end up in Inverness after all, making their own lives away from Callum's family. Despite Callum's claims that he could deal with that, Penelope knew he would be sad. He would be homesick.

It was up to her to see that it didn't happen.

PENELOPE WAS WOKEN the next morning by a hushed conversation. It was early, the sun barely risen, and she had tossed and turned for much of the night. Eventually, Callum had held her, his warm body a comfort, and she had reminded herself that she loved him and he loved her, and whatever came next they would weather together.

She lay still, attempting to listen to what was being said at the door to the room, but the voices were too low. It sounded like Callum and Luna, and it sounded like an argument. A quiet argument. Finally, the door closed and Callum returned to bed.

She sat up. "What was that about?"

He groaned. "My father has invited the neighbors over for luncheon."

"Oh." Was this a test? She assumed so. A test set for her by Maxwell. And if she failed . . .?

"Don't fash yourself," Callum said gently. "My father doesn't like our neighbors anyway."

"And yet he wanted a wife who would help him to fit in with others of his rank."

Callum groaned again. "I wish we had gone somewhere else instead of here. I thought . . . I hoped my father would be prepared to accept our marriage. He is a stubborn man."

"He is disappointed," Penelope said. "I understand that."

"I don't want you to feel you have to prove anything. Not to me, anyway. I love you and we are wed, and nothing will change that. Just because my father has some bee in his bonnet about us rising to the top, like we're swimming in a dish of cock-a-leekie . . .That's soup, my love, and Maxwell was never one for it anyway, so why—"

"MacKenzie," she put a stop to his rambling. "I think I understand your father. I can accept that I am not the wife he wanted for his son and heir. I think I am up for the challenge he has set me. At least let me *try*."

He looked up at her with shining eyes. "You are a bonny woman, my wife," he said in a low, gravelly voice. "A brave and wonderful woman."

She smiled and rumpled his hair. He was letting it grow again, the curls poking up in all directions, just the way she liked it. "We can always go back to London," she said.

"No, not London," he said. Then added hastily, in case he had offended her, "I don't mind a visit now and then, to see your brother and my aunt, but not to live."

"No, it does not suit you," she agreed fondly. "I think Bonnyrigg does. Since we arrived, you seem to . . . glow."

Which was all the more reason for her to win over Maxwell.

Callum wrapped his arms around her and drew her down, kissing her long and passionately. "If I am glowing," he whispered, "it is because my fairy wife has put a spell on me."

She laughed. "You do talk nonsense. Now kiss me again. Let's make the most of this comfy bed. I have become used to making love in far less comfortable places."

"Hmm, that reminds me," he grinned wickedly, "I have a few places in mind . . ."

CHAPTER TWENTY-SIX

D ESPITE HIS CALM demeanor in front of Penelope, Callum was angry with his father. He had hoped for more, and that Maxwell was behaving in such a stubborn, grumpy manner disappointed him. As for this luncheon . . . he wished they were not sitting down with their neighbors. He had hoped that they would refuse, but of course they were curious about Penelope, even Sir Hector who had sworn he would not enter Bonnyrigg again after Luna's outburst about the oatcakes. Penelope seemed to think this was some sort of test set by his father, and Callum feared she was right.

"Could Maxwell not have waited until we had settled in?" he demanded of Angus, when they met in the forest.

Angus looked as if he was having trouble keeping the smile off his face. Being married to Selina suited him. But he tried for a serious expression for Callum's sake.

"Your father is giving your wife a chance to prove herself. If she fails then mabbe you could say at least she tried. Luna likes her, as do your brothers and sister. As far as I can see, 'tis only Maxwell who is the thorn in the stocking."

Callum gave a gloomy nod. His mother and siblings did appear to like Penelope. They treated her as one of them, which she told him she found delightful. "It makes me feel like I have a family at last," she explained.

He understood. She had been alone after her parents died, and then estranged from Mortimer. Naturally, she was enjoying being part of a larger family.

He just wished Maxwell would stop being such a prick.

Last night at dinner, his father hadn't been at the end of the table as he usually was. The duke's chair had been empty and his mother had explained he had business to attend to. But she had appeared to be worried. Callum had wanted to go and hunt him out and give him a piece of his mind, but he knew that would only make it worse. He decided he would wait until after luncheon today and then he would make it clear to Maxwell that he was not going to stand for his behavior. If he did not stop treating Penelope like an unwelcome guest, then they would leave.

All very grand, but he had the sinking feeling that Maxwell would think that was a good idea. Perhaps that was what he wanted? Would he go so far as to disinherit his eldest son just because he did not marry as he had been instructed?

"Let the lassie do her thing," Angus said now. "She is good at soothing ruffled feathers."

Callum agreed, but in his mind he was already deciding whereabouts in Inverness they could find a suitable house.

THE LONG DINING table in the great hall was set with glassware and silverware, the many-branched candelabra in its center. There was even some greenery but thankfully no stuffed boars. Callum knew word had got back to his family about that because Rory had shared his thoughts on it and Cat had giggled uncontrollably.

It made him wonder why Penelope wanted a family like his. There were times when he could have happily done without them.

The neighbors were treated to sherry before the meal, and Sir Hector pulled a face as he finished it off in one gulp, the tiny glass even smaller in his great paw. "What's wrong with whisky?" he demanded. "We are real men here."

"Some of us are women," Luna retorted, glaring back.

Callum asked himself again why on earth his father cared what such fellows thought, but he knew why. He had been told often enough. Maxwell was ambitious for his family, and he needed powerful friends rather than enemies if he was to see the MacKenzies rise higher. It had always been his dream, and made all the stronger by the stinging comments he had received from others who thought him too lowborn to hold the position of duke.

"The fools say I do not deserve the title," he had said bitterly. "One day they will change their tune."

Penelope stood at Callum's side and was introduced, curtsying prettily. She was a strikingly beautiful woman, but he worried that her looks might be held against her. People might say he had been blinded by her beauty and married her despite his father's opposition.

"Ye are from London then?" Hector said disparagingly. "I do no' see the sense of the place myself. Why go south of the border when we have the grandest towns here? Edinburgh for instance. London is nothing to Edinburgh."

Penelope listened with polite attention. "If that is so, then surely you have much to teach the people of London," she said earnestly.

Hector eyed her doubtfully. "Do you think they would listen?"

"I think they would. Although . . ." she hesitated. "Your accent might cause them some difficulties. You may have to speak very slowly, Sir Hector, because Londoners are rather slow learners."

His clever wife had said the right thing, and Sir Hector looked pleased as he took his place at the table with the others. The courses were brought forth, *proper* servings Callum was glad to see, and he helped himself to seconds.

"Have ye cooked the oatcakes the way they should be cooked?" Hector said at one point, reminding them again of his falling out with Luna.

"I have them cooked the way they are always cooked," Luna retorted, setting down her cutlery with a clatter.

"I have heard your oatcakes are the best in Scotland, Your Grace," Penelope bravely spoke up. "But then I know so little about them. Tell me, Sir Hector, how do yours differ?"

Hector gave her a considering look. "I don't quite know. My cook is the one who makes them and she assures me they are the best."

"Oh. Perhaps she could show me."

"Ye want my cook to show you how to make oatcakes?" Hector asked, surprised and with a touch of cynicism.

"If she wouldn't mind," Penelope said deferentially. "Then I could taste them and decide for myself. Her Grace wouldn't mind, would you, Your Grace?" She looked at Luna with a smile.

"Of course not!" Luna declared, happy to join in. "I will rise to the challenge, Sir Hector. What say you? Are you brave enough to pit your cakes against mine?"

Hector seemed to be searching for the trap. "Aye, verra well. No tricks, mind."

"I do not need any," Luna said sweetly. "My oatcakes are the best by far."

Callum looked doubtfully at his wife, and she gave him a wink. He remembered Angus's saying he should trust her, but it was difficult to do so when there seemed to be so much at stake at this blasted luncheon.

The conversation turned to other matters. Maxwell spoke of the sheep owned by his neighbors encroaching on his borders. "I do not mind them," he said, "but they take the land that feeds my tenants." Hector thought the opposite, that there was good money to be made from the beasts. They argued, but to Callum's relief, it did not become hostile.

After the meal, they sat about the great fire, the men drinking

Maxwell's whisky, and the women chatting about children and their households.

"The ladies do not withdraw at Bonnyrigg?" Penelope asked curiously. "In London, the ladies withdraw to a separate room and leave the men to their talk."

The room fell silent. "We do not withdraw at Bonnyrigg," Luna said with a decided snap. "Not while I have breath in my body."

"We ladies have just as much to say as the menfolk," Cat spoke up, clearly echoing something her mother had told her. "We want our part in any decisions that have to be made."

Luna gave her a pleased nod. "We are equal partners here."

"Oh, I agree," Penelope said with feeling. "I always thought it very unfair. An old fashioned practice. This is so much better. My mother always wanted to stay to hear what was being spoken about," she frowned, "and perhaps to stop him making another unwise investment, but my father was a conventional sort of man."

Luna watched her curiously. "Your parents are in London?"

"No, no, that is . . ." Penelope swallowed and Callum reached for her hand—he was seated beside her.

"Penelope's parents were killed in an accident ten years ago. She and her brother were left orphans."

Sir Hector was quick to respond. "What sort of accident? A shooting accident? My brother died when one o' his guests shot him instead o' the grouse. Bloody fool."

"It was a coaching accident," Penelope said. "The coach rolled over and they were killed. My brother was only eight years old, and I had care of him."

Luna exchanged a glance with Maxwell. "You were barely a child yourself," she said with feeling. "Were you supported by other members of your family?"

Penelope seemed to be struggling with this subject and Callum wanted to put an end to it, but then he saw how those around them were hanging on her every word.

"My father had lost what money we had left through his bad investments, so we had no financial support. As for family . . . I have an uncle, but he is a selfish sort of man who did not want to be bothered with his sister's children. A friend of my father's stepped in and offered me assistance and I took it, to my cost, but what else was I to do?"

Penelope's cheeks were fiery red. Her meaning would not be clear to most of the guests here, but Callum was sure his parents knew exactly what she was saying. Jennie would have explained matters to them. He admired his wife's bravery in telling the truth when she could so easily have brushed it aside.

"Callum is so lucky." Penelope looked at him, love in her eyes, before turning to the rest of his family seated nearby. "If he needs help, he has you to ask. I am sure most of you here have families to depend on, and to love, and who love you. I do not know all of your circumstances, but I hope to. I had no one, and I still feel that loss. My brother was estranged and only lately has reunited with me. I have Callum to thank for that," and no one could doubt she meant it.

Callum sought to lighten the conversation before they were all in tears. "He was a wee nightmare when I first met him," he said, "but I quite like him now."

That made them laugh and Callum felt the mood shift. Even his father was watching Penelope as if she was no longer his enemy.

"You have a brother?" Cat's blue eyes were wide. "Why didn't you bring him with you?"

Penelope bit her lip so Callum answered for her. "He did not want to come."

"Then you must write to him," Maxwell declared loudly. "Tell him he must visit as soon as possible. It is important to have your family around you."

"But aren't we Penelope's family now?" Cat asked innocently, eyes even wider.

Maxwell stared at her a moment like he might reprimand her,

and then he shook his head in defeat. "Aye, we are," he agreed.

Callum felt such a wave of relief wash over him. He lifted Penelope's hand to his lips, silently thanking her, and she gave him a shaky smile before turning her full attention on Maxwell.

"Thank you, Your Grace," she said, heartfelt. "After my parents died, I longed for someone to say those words to me."

Hector raised his glass, getting rather unsteadily to his feet. "To the boy's wife! Even if she is an English lassie, she is one of us!"

They all drank, heartily echoing the toast.

Later, when the guests had gone, Luna and Maxwell invited Penelope to walk with them in the walled garden. Cat and her stripy kitten—more of a cat now—joined them, while Callum dawdled behind, listening to the sound of their voices. His father was telling the story of Callum running off to live in a tree, and Penelope was smiling as if she had never heard it before, and then Luna told the story of her meeting with his father, and Penelope was laughing.

Callum heard footsteps behind him and turned to find his brother Rory, casting an interested glance over the domestic scene.

"She is quite a woman, your wife," he said. "Well done, Callum. And thank you. Our father has been telling me that it was up to me to bring home a suitable wife since you had failed."

"Has he?" Callum shot Maxwell a dark look.

"Yes, but my point is, he is won over. I will be able to remain fancy free."

"Don't count on it," Callum said. "He'll want us all married to 'suitable' partners. It's your turn now."

Rory laughed. "I'll never marry."

Callum looked across at his wife. "Then you're a fool. I heartily recommend it."

But he could see Rory did not believe him. Oh well, one day his brother would fall in love and then it would be Callum's turn to laugh.

CHAPTER TWENTY-SEVEN

S ELINA WAS WASHING at the basin and was not aware of her husband's arrival in their room. Not until he caught her around the waist and squeezed.

"Angus!" she scolded him.

"Can I not cuddle my wife?" he asked her, a little hurt, and stepping back as she turned to face him.

They had been married for several weeks now. Selina remembered their handfasting ceremony with joy, and their arrival at Bonnyrigg. The MacKenzies had been kind to her, even Maxwell, and she had taken her place as Penelope's maid. Thank goodness her friend had been accepted, too—some days she shone with happiness.

Only now there was a complication and Selina didn't know what to do about it. She wanted to protect Angus from disappointment, if matters did not go as they should, but instead of protecting him, she was pushing him away. This was the second time today she had scolded him for nothing at all. No wonder he was hurt and confused.

"Selina," he said, and she could see the worry in his eyes as he held out his hand. "What is it? Are you no' happy here?"

He would offer to go elsewhere, tear up his roots for her sake, and she could not have that.

"I am happy," she said, and took his hand in hers. "Angus, it isn't that."

He shook his head. "'Tis something, I know it. Tell me what

is wrong, so I can make it right."

Of course he would say that. He had promised at their hand-fasting that he would make her happy.

"I am having a baby and I'm too old!" She wailed the words. "I am forty, Angus, and I'm sure it will go wrong, and you will be so upset with me, and . . ."

The rest of her words were smothered by his broad chest as he held her, rocking her close. After a time, when she was calm, he said, "It is grand news, aye, it is. Mabbe it will not finish well, but I willna think of that, my love. I will just be happy for each day that passes."

"Yes," she agreed. He was right. What was the use in expecting the worst instead of taking each day as it came? She sniffed and let him wipe her cheeks dry of tears.

"'Tis not what I expected," he admitted. "I thought you'd decided Bonnyrigg was no' for you, or worse, *I* was no' for you."

"Angus, I could never not want you," she murmured, kissing his whiskery cheek.

"Then let us enjoy this moment," he said firmly. "I do not believe in borrowing trouble."

Distracted, he looked out of the window at the sky. "It will rain soon," he said, with the certainty of someone who knew the weather well. "The home Callum made for his creatures has a leak in it. He has found dry corners for most of them, apart from two." He cocked an eyebrow at her. "Do you want the squirrel or the crow?"

Selina giggled. "The crow, please."

She had seen all the creatures now, and the crow was less trouble.

"What do you think Penelope will think when her husband arrives in their bedchamber with the squirrel?"

Selina laughed out loud. "She will forgive him," she said, "because she loves him."

Angus looked uncertain. "Will we tell people?" he asked. "About the baby? Luna is good with such things, you know.

Women come to her for help."

Selina had not known that and was glad to hear it. "Not just yet," she said. "I want to enjoy it with you."

He kissed her cheek. "Thank you," he whispered.

PENELOPE RESTED HER head on her husband's chest and closed her eyes. She was happy and contented. Callum's parents had accepted her. They were kindhearted people and her sad story had won them around, although Callum said it was her handling of the oatcake situation that had done the trick. Whatever the reason, she was determined she would continue to prove herself a valuable asset when it came to Maxwell's ambitions for his family.

This was only the beginning, and she was looking forward to the challenges ahead.

"I know I said we could live in Inverness," Callum said, his voice rumbling in his chest, "but I am glad we don't have to go."

"I am glad, too."

Outside, a summer storm was pelting rain against the windows and bending the trees in the forest. Callum had been out to check on his creatures, and she suspected he had brought some of them into the bedchamber, but she wasn't sure she wanted to know. There was a rustling beneath the bed that sounded very suspicious.

"You know it is not socially acceptable to share your bed with animals," she said. "Unless they are cats or dogs, I suppose, and even then . . ."

"Ah, Penelope, I could not leave them outside in this. There is a leak in the roof of the home I made for them."

"And who are 'they'? Please, not another mouse."

He laughed. "Remember that night? I should tell Rory, he will enjoy the laugh."

"Did I hear right? Is Rory going to London to stay with your Aunt Jennie?"

"Yes, he is." Callum looked up at the canopy above the bed. "I told him you could give him some lessons in etiquette but he said as he wasn't hanging out for a wife, he did not need any."

"Then why is he going?"

Callum guffawed. "He doesn't want me to be the only one to conquer the English."

Penelope could have said some things about that, but she decided not to. She snuggled closer. "I am so glad your aunt employed me. I cannot imagine my life without you in it."

"Nor me."

He bent his head to kiss her, and their kisses occupied them for some time.

"Selina is very happy with her new husband," she said at last, sleepily. "I am glad I did not have to leave her behind."

"It has worked out verra well for us all," Callum said smugly, as if it was all his doing.

There was that rustle again, and he flicked her a nervous glance. "'Tis only the blind squirrel," he soothed her. "She was afraid, and I could not leave her out there. Tomorrow I will build them a better place, I promise."

"I will hold you to that," Penelope said sternly.

"The headmistress voice," Callum groaned and rolled over, his mouth on her throat, and then he began kissing his way south.

"I cannot have you disobeying the rules," she went on even more sternly, but she was trying not to laugh.

He pressed his face between her legs, his tongue busy, and she arched up with a gasp of pleasure. No more words were spoken as he brought matters to a pleasurable conclusion.

Penelope forgot about the animal under the bed, drawing his face up to hers again, as he pushed himself inside her, deep and deeper still.

They had spoken about children, and it was something she dearly wanted, but for now she was happy just to have Callum as her husband and to settle into life at Bonnyrigg.

Who would have thought that she would be so happy? The girl who had taken an improper proposal for the sake of her brother, and then fought her way back to respectability. The girl who had taught the unteachable how to succeed in society, and married her student despite the reasons she should not.

The woman who was so loved.

Callum was looking down at her, amusement warming his dark eyes. "Where did you go?" he asked.

Penelope stretched up to kiss his lips. "Nowhere. I am right here where I belong."

CHAPTER TWENTY-EIGHT

THE FIRST YEAR of married life for Callum and Penelope, and their first year at Bonnyrigg, had flown by with so many joys to celebrate. Despite her doubts, Selina had sailed through her pregnancy and birthed a healthy baby. Now here she was, holding the child wrapped in a fine new blanket, as Angus leaned protectively close, smiling like the proud father he was. Callum smiled too at the sight of them. They were both besotted, and the guests in the little chapel cooed and sighed at the sight as the sun shone through the stained-glass window. This baptism was the first for Bonnyrigg for some time, and everyone was making the most of it.

Penelope had told Callum that Selina still called her baby a miracle, and Callum laughed and wondered aloud what they would call it when the next one arrived.

"I think one is probably enough," she had replied, grimacing at the memory of her friend in labor.

Callum placed a gentle hand on his wife's belly, which had grown rather large in the past few weeks. According to Luna, their baby was due very soon now. Maxwell was worse than Callum when it came to worrying about it. He was forever insisting Penelope sit down or setting a stool for her to rest her feet on. He would have rubbed them, too, if Callum had not taken on that role.

No one would ever have believed his father had ever been against their marriage.

"Where is Rory?" Maxwell said now, frowning about at the congregation.

"He promised he would be home for the birth of Penelope's baby," Luna whispered.

The MacKenzies' standing had improved since Penelope had come to stay. She had the knack of drawing the neighbors together, and the oatcake competition had been so successful it was now to run every year, with contestants coming from near and far. Sir Hector's and Luna's cakes had been declared a draw, but they both vowed to win next time.

Callum loved his wife more each day, and the thought of their child made him smile every time he thought of it. He had been worried at first, Penelope was so small, but his mother had reassured him.

"I am small, too," she had reminded him, "and I have three strapping sons and a daughter."

So Callum had set aside his fears to enjoy this special time in their lives.

The minister caught his eye, and he rose to go to Angus. He was to be godfather to the baby and was determined to take his role very seriously. Godmother was Penelope, but due to her condition, Cat was standing in for her.

"Oh, look at her tiny fingers," his sister fussed, peering down at the child. She smiled at him shyly, "I can't wait until your baby is born, Callum. Will it be a boy, do you think? Father hopes for a boy."

"Well, Father has no say in this," Callum said, "and I will be happy either way."

"There can never be enough girls at Bonnyrigg," Cat announced seriously. "That is what our mother says."

Callum looked toward the people packed into the pews. Penelope was smiling in the dreamy way that meant she was feeling their baby move inside her, and Maxwell and Luna were smiling at each other. Donal was there, looking miserable since his true love had left for London.

Only Rory was missing. Callum wanted to see him, if only so he could scoff at his brother's assertion that he would never marry, but he was genuinely happy that Rory the rake was finally settled.

Callum found himself remembering the day he had left all of this behind to ride to London, and how he had been determined not to enjoy himself and certainly not to find a wife. How differently it had turned out. How glad he now was that he had set off for the south.

His gaze searched out Penelope again, only to find her looking straight at him. Her eyes were open wide, their silvery color very evident, and then she smiled. "Callum!" she cried out. "The baby is coming!"

And everything turned to chaos.

PENELOPE SAT PROPPED up with pillows in the bed, blind to everything but the baby inside her wanting to get out. Selina had told her it was a "trifle" painful, and she had seen for herself how much hard work it was to deliver a baby, but she still hadn't understood the full extent of it. Callum was outside—she could hear his voice as he demanded entry—but Luna had told him to stay put.

"Can I see her now?" he kept asking.

"Your mother will not allow it," Maxwell had replied.

"I cannot bear to think of her in pain," Callum had wailed.

"Your mother will see her through, son," Maxwell had soothed.

Luna's calming voice brought Penelope back to the bed.

"The duke wants an heir," Penelope gasped.

Luna snorted. "The duke will have to make do. None of us care if it is a boy or a girl, my dear, and we will love it just as we love you."

Penelope thought that was perhaps the nicest thing she had ever heard. She wanted to answer, to say she loved the MacKenzies too, but the next moment the baby decided it was ready to be born.

Sometime later she lay, washed clean and wearing a fresh nightgown, the child swaddled in a fine blanket, awaiting her husband.

When Callum arrived, his hair looked like he had been tearing it out, and his eyes were wide as he hurried to her side. "I am so glad . . . so proud . . . so grateful," he said, but couldn't seem to finish a sentence.

Penelope received his kisses and let him hold her, carefully, before she said, "You haven't asked about the baby."

His eyes widened. "The baby is well?"

"Of course," she soothed him. "I meant you haven't asked whether it is a boy or a girl."

Callum buried his face against her neck. "Tell me then," he said, "but the truth is I dinna care, my love. It is our child and I will love it, but I am just so happy all is well."

Maxwell peered around the door jamb, looking as frazzled as his son. Luna waved him in. "Have you forgotten?" she asked him gently. "You were always beside yourself when our children were born."

"Aye, I had forgotten," he admitted. "And I find I do not care if 'tis a boy or a girl. 'Tis a MacKenzie, and our dear daughter-in-law is healthy and strong, and that's what counts."

Despite feeling rather tired, Penelope beamed. She had won Maxwell over long ago, but hearing him admit it still warmed her to the very cockles of her heart.

The door opened again and Cat came in, her flaming hair down, in her nightgown. Her excited gaze went to the bundle in Penelope's arms. "Oh!" she whispered. "Please tell me 'tis a girl, Pen."

"You have your wish," Penelope said, smiling.

"A wee girl!" Callum cried. "Did you hear, Father?"

Maxwell reached out a gentle finger and stroked the baby's cheek. "Aye, I did. We are indeed blessed."

Penelope allowed their voices to drift around her, half dozing as she lay, surrounded by her loving family, with her husband at her side, and her daughter in her arms. Life was very good, and it could only get better.

About the Author

Sara Bennett is an Australian bestselling author of Historical Romance. She has written many books set in various time periods—Medieval, Regency and Victorian—as well as Paranormal Romance under the name Sara Mackenzie.

She started her career writing under the penname Deborah Miles for Mills & Boon. Her books have been published by Avon/Harper Collins, and are available worldwide. She has also written numerous Australian Women's Fiction books as Kaye Dobbie. Currently she alternates between publishing independently and with traditional publishers.

Sara has been a finalist for the RITA award (Romance Writers of America) and the RUBY (Romance Writers of Australia).

Sara lives in Victoria, Australia, in an old house in a goldrush town, with her husband and two important cats. She would love to spend more time in the garden but there are just too many stories to be written.